FLIGHT RISK

UNIVERSITY OF CALGARY
Press

FLIGHT RISK

A PLAY
by Meg Braem

ESSAYS
by William John Pratt and
by David B. Hogan and Philip D. St. John

DIRECTOR'S NOTES
by Samantha MacDonald

Brave & Brilliant Series
ISSN 2371-7238 (Print) ISSN 2371-7246 (Online)

University of Calgary Press
2500 University Drive NW
Calgary, Alberta
Canada T2N 1N4
press.ucalgary.ca

LIBRARY AND ARCHIVES CANADA CATALOGUING IN PUBLICATION

Title: Flight risk / a play by Meg Braem ; essays by William John Pratt and by David B. Hogan
    and Philip D. St. John ; director's notes by Samantha MacDonald.
Names: Braem, Meg, author.
Series: Brave & brilliant series ; no. 34.
Description: Series statement: Brave & brilliant series ; no. 34 | Includes bibliographical
    references.
Identifiers: Canadiana (print) 20230227678 | Canadiana (ebook) 20230227686 | ISBN
    9781773854724 (softcover) | ISBN 9781773854717 (hardcover) | ISBN 9781773854731 (PDF)
    | ISBN 9781773854748 (EPUB)
Subjects: LCGFT: Drama.
Classification: LCC PS8603.R333 F55 2023 | DDC C812/.6—dc23

The University of Calgary Press acknowledges the support of the Government of Alberta
through the Alberta Media Fund for our publications. We acknowledge the financial support
of the Government of Canada. We acknowledge the financial support of the Canada Council
for the Arts for our publishing program.

Printed and bound in Canada by Marquis
♻ This book is printed on Enviro book natural paper

Editing and copyediting by Naomi K. Lewis
Cover art: Colourbox 7490645 and 1818670
Cover design, page design, and typesetting by Melina Cusano

Contents

FOREWORD

By Meg Braem

.

Where do stories come from?

This story came out of a bad year.

In the span of six months, I watched my father die, began to suffer excruciating headaches, got fired from my job, went blind in one eye, and lost the ability to walk more than ten feet without falling over. It felt like the earth was trying to shake me off. I was thirty-two years old. I thought, "If this adulthood, I'm not gonna make it."

After being sent to a psychologist because my doctor thought that I was just sad that my dad died, and a trip to the emergency room, where the only diagnostic I was offered was a pregnancy test, a neurologist discovered that I was suffering from a massive multiple sclerosis (MS) flareup. I received a horse's dose of steroids and went home to wait for the inflammation in my brain to calm down.

They called it convalescing, but really, it was waiting . . . waiting to see if things would get better — or worse. Waiting to see if I would end up in a wheelchair. Waiting to see if I would be half blind forever. Waiting for the other shoe to drop. I slept a lot, mostly on my couch. After three months, my eyesight came back, I could walk better, and I started getting bored lying around the house.

I remember going out for the first time and someone asking me what I'd been up to. I didn't know what to tell them. People kept asking the same question, in different ways. Sometimes I would say, "Oh, you know, writing." Sometimes I would try out the truth. A friend happened to be in town for a few days, and we decided to meet for breakfast. We hadn't seen each other for close to two years. When she asked me how I was doing, I told her. As I watched the blood drain from her face, I realized that I was being scary. My year of loss and sickness was a terrible affront to the peaceful, planned, and not-too-unpleasant lives we'd both expected to live. That year at a Christmas party, a friend sat me down to ask if I'd ever thought about using essential oils to cure my MS. She thought frankincense and myrrh would be most effective due to their ability to travel through the blood/brain barrier. How seasonal. I swallowed my mini quiche and asked snarkily if it had been written about in the *Lancet*. Another acquaintance told me to plan for a big hiking trip come summer. I confessed that my legs weren't dependable enough. I wouldn't be able to hike anymore. They looked at me and said, "You won't let that happen." The truth was, I didn't let any of it happen, and yet it did. I needed to be with people who understood that.

Since I didn't have a job and was too scared to get one for fear that I would be a burden and consequently fired again, I audited a history of medicine course at the University of Calgary. I hid amongst the med students. I liked that no one knew anything about me. I liked that no one would notice I was different from before. I liked the directness in terms of talking about illness. I liked being with people who would have to confront death in one way or another. If all of this sounds like it was a profound bummer, it wasn't. It was refreshing to be with people who could at least admit to being mortal.

I read about sickness, aging, and end of life. I started to visit long-term care homes to talk with the elderly. Some people told me about their daily experiences of hating the food and feeling dismissed by the staff, the small agonies of losing control of one's life. These were people who had lived active, rich lives and weren't sure who they were anymore. I could relate. Mostly though, people told stories. I met ninety-year-old tail gunner Bob Petersen at the

Bomber Command Museum in Nanton, Alberta. When I asked what it was like to be on a bomb run, he replied, "cold." When I got home, I researched him and found a video produced by his care home. In the video he recounted how he was once grounded due to an injury, and his crew had to fly a mission without him. They never came back. I couldn't stop thinking about it. How many people had stories like this? How many of those stories were being heard?

William John Pratt's chapter provides historical context for Hank's war years, stitching together the stories of many young Canadian men who flew with Bomber Command. Pratt shows that there were all too many stories like Hank's. Airmen faced their own deaths every night they flew. Like Bob Petersen, they left many of their compatriots behind. Some who survived the war found that everything after that intense period seemed mundane.

Hank serves as an amalgam of wartime memories; however, another historical study suggests that the fictional Hank is not typical in his failure to age well. David Hogan and Philip D. St. John's chapter traces the long-term medical follow-up study of a group of air force veterans. The Manitoba Follow Up Study originally recruited some four thousand air force veterans in the 1940s. By 2018, only 137 of them were still living. The loss of these men and their memories of the war, not to mention the memories of the rest of their lives, is saddening, yet the study does offer some positive findings. Since 1996, the majority of the participants who responded said they had aged successfully. If the fictional Hank had been a participant, his pessimism and negative outlook would have placed him in the minority. Most real air force veterans who lived to their seventies were doing well, despite the inevitable aging process.

I wrote *Flight Risk* because I needed to talk about mortality. Since early 2020, as the coronavirus pandemic has threatened our lives and livelihoods, we have all been reminded of our humanity. Overnight we became frightened that the very air we breathed would kill us. There was no contingency plan for COVID-19. As we struggled to adapt, or 'pivot' as became the oft-repeated vernacular, we were reminded of the most vulnerable in our communities. Outbreaks in long-term care facilities across the country were swift and ruthless. News cycles were filled with the numbers: of long-term care homes effected, of case counts, and of deaths. The figures were staggeringly high. As the same story was repeated across the country in 2020, however, the tale began to lose its teeth. It wasn't news anymore that the elderly were suffering. Eventually press attention shifted elsewhere, and the story faded away, sadly rearing its head once again in early 2022. After a long, numbing pandemic with a news cycle dominated by epidemiological statistics, individual stories were lost.

Feeling hopeless is a common condition in a world with so many unknowns, but there are positive initiatives that predate the pandemic, committed to telling the stories that may have gone unheard. I recently had the pleasure of working with the GeriActors, an internationally renowned Edmonton-based company creating and promoting seniors' and intergenerational theatre. Since 2001, seniors from the Edmonton area, along with students and alumni from the University of Alberta, have collaborated as company members. Founder and artistic director, David Barnet, uses the practice of creative aging to encourage older adults to express themselves. The "Geris," as they are known, currently range from sixty-five to ninety years old, with collaborators averaging about twenty-two.

Sick + Twisted is a theatre company dedicated to creating work exploring the experience of living with a disability. Sick + Twisted's vision reminds us that "all performance is rooted in the body and much exploration of the human condition is rooted in the recognition of the fragility of this flesh."[1] I reached out to Sick + Twisted artistic director Debbie Patterson in 2021, when she was nominated for the Gina Wilkinson Prize. Debbie's biography relayed that she found out she had multiple sclerosis after going blind at a writers' retreat. I wrote to her to thank her for being so open about her disease. I confessed for the first time to a stranger that I, too, had MS. Debbie wrote me back and told me that I'd be surprised by how many people are dealing with invisible illnesses.

People who I'd never think could be ill, people who I work with right now. I felt embarrassed and relieved when I read that, the thing that I've been carrying around, my deepest darkest secret, was quite normal. It made me wish I'd known and could share stories with those people. It made me want to hear people tell their stories. In his book *The Wounded Storyteller*, Arthur W. Frank calls on us to "witness" our illnesses, aging, and humanity so that we might share those experiences with others.[2] This storytelling takes an isolating experience and creates compassion and community. We must realize that if age and sickness remind us of death, they should also remind us of life.

FLIGHT RISK

A Play by Meg Braem

Playwright's Notes

When the phone rang after midnight, we all braced ourselves for the news. We had spent the evening at the hospital with chairs pulled close, sipping scotch brought over by the doctor (who stayed to listen) while my father held court from his deathbed. By this time, he was nothing but teeth and eyebrows, but that night he hosted us with a big smile and shining eyes. He held his drink high, commented on how smooth it was, and announced that this was a good day to die. The call was expected, but not the caller . . . it wasn't a nurse telling us he had slipped away in the night; it was my dad. He was high on morphine and damn mad he wasn't dead yet. He died two weeks later after losing his ability to speak.

Even after he couldn't speak, I could hear him, and I started writing down his voice, because I was scared that I would forget. I wanted to be around people who knew about mortality and weren't afraid to talk about it. I started visiting nursing homes. I spoke to a Royal Canadian Air Force vet after a Remembrance Day Ceremony in his assisted living lodge. I went to the Bomber Command Museum and met ninety-year-old tail gunner Bob Petersen. I received a copy of tail gunner Doug Curtis' personal chronicle of his war experience. The character of Hank is a composite of all these men. Writing down a voice so as not to forget led me to hearing more voices — all of which I am honoured to remember.

Characters

HANK DUNFIELD: 99-year-old veteran of the Second World War. Former tail gunner in the Royal Canadian Air Force (Bomber Command).

SARAH BAKER: Mid-twenties nursing student.

KATHLEEN SHORE: Mid-fifties registered nurse. Nursing supervisor at Ponderosa Pine Lodge Seniors Care Centre.

Setting

1. Ponderosa Pine Lodge Seniors Care Centre.
2. A field, 3 kilometres from Ponderosa Pine Lodge.

SCENE 1

A field. Early morning. The first sounds of birds can be heard as the dark fades into a sunrise. Using a walker, HANK *walks laboriously out into the grass, wearing a sleeping gown and slippers. He reaches the perfect spot and looks up at the sky.*

SCENE 2

Three days later. HANK *lies tucked into his bed in a single room.* KATHLEEN *enters, followed by* SARAH.

KATHLEEN: [*Upon entering*] He was found two days ago, wandering in a field about three kilometres from the lodge. He spent the night in the cold, but other than a slight bruise on his shin, he seems to be in good condition.

HANK: I'm fine.

KATHLEEN: We're very thankful he was found alive.

HANK: I said I was fine.

KATHLEEN: I'd like you to meet Mr. Henry Dunfield.

[*SARAH puts her hand out.*]

SARAH: Nice to meet you.

[*HANK stares straight ahead.*]

I'm Sarah.

[*HANK continues to stare at the wall.*]

KATHLEEN: I let him know you were coming. [*To HANK*] Remember, we talked about Sarah?

SARAH: That's okay. Maybe he forgot.

HANK: Haven't forgot anything. [*Looks at KATHLEEN*] She has.

SARAH: Oh.

KATHLEEN: Mr. Dunfield prefers to be called —

HANK: Name's Hank. Been Hank since the war.

KATHLEEN: Hank fought in the Second World War.

HANK: Tail gunner, number 419, Moose Squadron.

KATHLEEN: Hank, I want you to meet Sarah. She will be coming to the lodge three times a week and will be able to make sure you're comfortable.

HANK: What a drain on taxpayer's money.

SARAH: I'm here to help you.

HANK: You're here to make sure I don't run off again.

KATHLEEN: I'd hardly call it running off.

HANK: It's all in the rhythm. A walker can get a good clip with the right rhythm.

KATHLEEN: Sarah is a nursing student. She's going to be doing her practicum here at Ponderosa Pine Lodge.

HANK: I said I was fine.

KATHLEEN: You could have fallen.

HANK: But I didn't.

KATHLEEN: But you could have. [*To SARAH*] Hank is what we call a 'flight risk.' He has a tendency to wander off the grounds in the middle of the night. It's extremely dangerous. Residents can become disoriented and get lost.

HANK: I wasn't lost.

KATHLEEN: Hank is a very special resident here at the lodge. He's about to have his one-hundredth birthday!

HANK: If I make it that long.

KATHLEEN: You're a tough old bird. You'll make it.

SARAH: One hundred! Wow!

HANK: [*Sarcastic*] Weehoo.

KATHLEEN: Why don't I give you two a few minutes to get to know each other? [*Checks time*] I'll be back at 8:45 with your meds.

[*KATHLEEN gathers her clipboard and takes a few steps towards the door.*]

Is there anything I can get either of you while I'm out?

SARAH: I'm fine.

HANK: A piece of pie would hit the spot.

KATHLEEN: You know you can't.

HANK: One piece of pie isn't going to kill me.

KATHLEEN: It's up to me to see you make that one-hundredth birthday. Anything else?

HANK: If you find a reasonable facsimile for something palatable, I wouldn't say no.

KATHLEEN: I'll keep my eye out.

HANK: Everything here tastes like cardboard that's been left out in the rain.

KATHLEEN: You two have fun.

[*KATHLEEN exits. Awkward silence fills the room. SARAH looks around.*]

SARAH: I like your room.

HANK: What colour would you call it?

SARAH: Ahh, purplish brown.

HANK: It's puce.

SARAH: . . . puce.

HANK: Like a blend of the words puke and puss. The colour is often described as that of an old bloodstain left on a sheet after many washes.

SARAH: I can see that, actually.

HANK: An old stain on an old sheet from an old life that's been crumpled up and thrown in the back of the closet.

SARAH: Did they do that on purpose?

HANK: God, no. I'm sure it was on sale at the hardware store.

SARAH: Oh.

[*Long beat*]

You seem pretty sharp.

HANK: And that surprises you.

SARAH: No, well, I just thought —

HANK: I have my moments. I sometimes forget where I am, but that might be a blessing.

SARAH: Everyone here seems nice.

HANK: They're not.

SARAH: Kathleen is very nice.

HANK: That one? She's a dictator. It's like living under Hitler.

SARAH: I'm sure it's not.

HANK: Look closer. She's even got the same moustache.

SARAH: She wants to make sure nothing happens to you.

HANK: Know what? Nothing ever does. Nothing happens. I sit here all day in an environment designed to stop anything from ever happening. This place is as much a nursery as a nursing home. We've been relegated to being infants again . . . and here you are, my very own nursemaid.

[KATHLEEN enters.]

KATHLEEN: How are we doing here?

SARAH: Uh —

KATHLEEN: [To HANK] I have a treat for you.

HANK: Pie?

KATHLEEN: There's a granola bar waiting for you in the dining hall with your medication.

HANK: A granola bar? Why does everything have to be multipurpose these days? Telephones that take pictures, two-in-one shampoos . . . a dessert that helps you take a crap. A treat has a single purpose: to be delicious.

KATHLEEN: There's one for you, too, Sarah, if you're hungry.

SARAH: . . . thanks.

KATHLEEN: [To HANK] I saw Reggie in the hallway. Should I tell him you don't want it?

[HANK flings off his blankets.]

HANK: You tell that bastard to get his own.

[*HANK struggles to stand and reach for his walker.* KATHLEEN *helps him rise and transfer over. She does the transfer with deft skill, making sure her feet are planted with one hand in his armpit and the other on the back of his waist.* SARAH *spots them awkwardly, as if to catch them when they fall. Once transferred,* SARAH *and* KATHLEEN *watch as he slowly leaves the room.*]

KATHLEEN: His bark is worse than his bite.

SARAH: Want me to help you with your rounds?

KATHLEEN: I think this is where you will be needed most.

SARAH: This floor?

KATHLEEN: This room. You'll spend your visits with Mr. Dunfield.

SARAH: I think I'm offending him by being here.

KATHLEEN: You don't offend him . . . you depress him.

SARAH: That's not any better.

KATHLEEN: We all depress him. He's depressed. Maybe you can find out how to snap him out of it.

SARAH: But I'm only here for a limited time.

KATHLEEN: We're planning a big birthday party for him. I have to figure out the catering, the decorations . . . just keep him busy.

SARAH: Look, I'm not going to be dealing with this sort of thing. I'm going to get a job in the E.R.

[*KATHLEEN has heard this before*]

I'm only here for three weeks.

KATHLEEN: Then you'll be here for the party. His birthday is on the fourth.

SARAH: . . . I didn't sign up for this.

KATHLEEN: But you signed up to be a nurse?

SARAH: . . . yes.

KATHLEEN: Then you signed up for a career of doing things you didn't sign up for. That's the job . . .

[*Checks watch.*]

I have a meeting with regional health.

[*She starts to go but turns back.*]

Oh, and Sarah?

SARAH: Yeah?

KATHLEEN: Your feet.

SARAH: My feet?

KATHLEEN: When you do a transfer, feet parallel and shoulder width apart . . . for your back.

SARAH: Right . . . thanks.

KATHLEEN: And see if you can find out Hank's favourite party food.

[*KATHLEEN exits. SARAH sits down on a chair and looks at the walls around her.*]

SARAH: Puce.

SCENE 3

Middle of the night. The Lodge is quiet. HANK appears wearing pajamas and slippers. He walks in a trance-like state (much like sleep walking), slowly making his way to the front door. He tries to open it, but finds it locked. He jiggles the handle, getting more and more anxious. The noise of the door banging alerts KATHLEEN, *who enters. She gently leads him back to his room, careful not to wake him.*

SCENE 4

SARAH *sits in* HANK's *room, waiting with medication and a bottle of water in her hands.* HANK *shuffles into the room.*

HANK: You're back.

SARAH: I am.

[SARAH *arranges the medication into a small plastic cup and pours a cup of water.* HANK *looks at his watch.*]

HANK: You're early.

SARAH: I had a doctor's appointment. His office is right around the corner.

HANK: What would someone your age want with a doctor?

SARAH: Just a checkup.

HANK: I hate doctors.

SARAH: So do I.

HANK: Already sounding like a nurse.

[HANK *positions himself on the bed and looks into his cup of medication. He begins to swallow the pills. As he does this,* SARAH *lifts a bottle of aspirin out of her purse and takes out four pills.* HANK *watches her quickly swallow them, drinking the rest of his water bottle. He lifts his pills out to her.*]

I'm full. You want mine?

SARAH: I get headaches.

HANK: Must be some headache.

SARAH: *[changing the subject]* What do you usually do on Wednesdays?

HANK: Same thing I do every other day.

SARAH: Which is what?

HANK: Nothing.

SARAH: Nothing?

HANK: Nothing.

[*Beat*]

SARAH: You must do something.

HANK: I watch TV.

SARAH: Do you have a favourite show?

HANK: No . . . I don't like TV.

SARAH: Then why do you watch it?

HANK: Because there's nothing else to do.

[*HANK picks up the remote and turns on the TV. He stares at the screen. There is an awkward silence.*]

SARAH: Hank?

HANK: Yeah?

SARAH: Can you turn it off?

HANK: Why?

SARAH: Because . . . because maybe I'm here other than just to keep tabs on you.

HANK: Oh yeah?

SARAH: Maybe I'd like to get to know you.

HANK: The chart on the end of the bed will tell you everything you need to know . . . when I take my medications, when I bathe, right down to when I'm scheduled to have a bowel movement.

SARAH: The real fifty shades of grey.

[*SARAH pulls a pack of cards out of her purse.*]

Do you like cards?

[*HANK turns off the TV and looks at her.*]

HANK: You know how to play crib?

SARAH: No.

HANK: Rummy?

SARAH: No.

[*Beat*]

Go fish?

HANK: [*Disgusted*] Please.

[*HANK picks up the remote to turn the TV back on. SARAH looks around the room and picks up a pamphlet that's been left on a side table.*]

SARAH: Activities Calendar. Ah, here we go . . . there's got to be something good in this . . . Wednesdays, morning . . . religious studies or drama club.

HANK: Aren't they the same thing?

SARAH: Hmm, okay, crafts section . . . Wednesdays . . .

HANK: I don't like crafts.

SARAH: Everyone likes crafts. Let's see here, [*reading*] "Enjoy the versatility and endless creativity of pipe cleaners."

HANK: I wonder what the ratio is of pipe cleaners in the world that are actually used for cleaning pipes.

[*SARAH turns the page and reads.*]

SARAH: "Create a card to let your family know how much you love them using the luminous quality of glitter."

HANK: Reggie made a Christmas card one year, left a trail of glitter around the lodge for months.

SARAH: You could still make a card.

HANK: Who would I give it to?

SARAH: Someone in your family? Kathleen said you have a son.

HANK: He doesn't deserve a card.

[*SARAH looks at the pamphlet. Her hands start to shake. HANK notices. SARAH tucks her hand in her pocket. They look at each other.*]

SARAH: Sorry.

HANK: Don't say sorry.

SARAH: Sorr — I must have had too much coffee this morning.

[*Changing the subject*]

Not all crafts are like this. Some are great. Wood working, building stuff. Is there anything you used to do as a hobby?

HANK: I made models years ago. There's one I started somewhere in the back of the closet but —

[*SARAH jumps up and opens his closet door.*]

What are you doing? I don't remember giving you permission to ransack my closet.

[*She starts digging through sweaters and other things.*]

SARAH: Maybe I can help. I used to make doll furniture.

HANK: This isn't doll furniture.

[*SARAH shifts boxes around in the closet, a small rabbit's foot tumbles out. SARAH shrieks.*]

SARAH: Ahhhh! A mouse!

[*HANK moves closer with his walker. He lifts the leg of the walker above the object to squash it. He stops just before making contact.*]

HANK: My god. I haven't seen this for a long time.

SARAH: What is it?

HANK: A rabbit's foot.

SARAH: Oh, gross.

HANK: It's not gross. It's lucky.

SARAH: Not for the rabbit.

[*SARAH reluctantly picks it up and gives it to HANK.*]

HANK: There wasn't an airman who didn't have something. You didn't fly without a charm to give you luck.

SARAH: You had that in the war?

HANK: Never flew without it. All the boys had something . . . a pocket watch, a picture, a small stuffed panda. Vic never got in that cockpit before pissing on the tailwheel first.

[*HANK examines the rabbit's foot.*]

This rabbit's foot kept me alive during some long nights in the air.

[*He hands it to* SARAH, *who reluctantly touches it.*]

That is one lucky rabbit's foot.

[*She puts it on the table.*]

SARAH: Let's just put it here for safekeeping.

[SARAH *returns to digging in the closet. She pulls out a box with a half-built model in it.*]

This it?

[*She digs through the box.*]

Oh, I see, it's a plane.
HANK: It's a Lanc.
SARAH: A what?
HANK: Lancaster bomber.
SARAH: This the kind of plane you flew?
HANK: Twenty-four missions.

[SARAH *pulls out pieces of the model.*]

SARAH: This should be easy.
HANK: A Lanc may be simple, but nothing about it is ever easy.

[*HANK rifles through the pieces of model.*]

Not easy to get off the ground at dusk with a belly full of bombs. Not easy to get back on the ground in a morning fog so thick you can't see the airfield till you hit it.

[*SARAH opens the glue.*]

SARAH: This glue is all dried up.

HANK: Mission grounded.

[*SARAH sits down, defeated. HANK is about to turn the television on again.*]

SARAH: I just thought we could do something . . . other than watching TV.

HANK: Would you like a peppermint?

SARAH: . . . Sure.

HANK: . . . On the dresser there.

[*SARAH lifts the lid of the candy dish and pops one in her mouth.*]

SARAH: Scotch mints.

HANK: A truly dignified candy.

[*SARAH passes him the dish. HANK takes a mint.*]

A Scotch mint softens in the mouth, unlike a candy cane.

SARAH: My sister and I used to suck on candy canes until they were razor sharp.

HANK: Candy canes are only truly enjoyed by felons in need of a shiv.

SARAH: What other foods do you like?

HANK: The liver and onions on Tuesdays is tolerable.

SARAH: Ewww. I didn't know people still ate that.

HANK: This generation doesn't know what it's missing. It's cheap, full of iron. Liver was a real treat when rations meant boiled greens and potatoes. I haven't eaten a Brussels sprout since 1945.

SARAH: Okay, but if you could have something fancy —

HANK: I don't need fancy.

SARAH: Okay, but say, say you were invited to a fancy dinner —

HANK: By who?

SARAH: I don't know, your family . . . your son.

HANK: He hasn't invited me anywhere in two years.

SARAH: Well, say you were being honoured . . .

[*She looks at the model parts.*]

Honoured for your . . . efforts in the war

HANK: The only thing they ever did was give us a fresh egg after a night of flying. The rest of the time we ate powdered eggs just like everyone else.

SARAH: Say there was a fancy dinner . . . champagne, hors d'oeuvres —

HANK: Blach! Hors d'oeuvres! I never understood why everyone got so uppity about little things that look like they died at birth served on toast. When I want a meal, I want a meal. A steak cooked exactly the time it takes to smoke two cigarettes. A pie for dessert, pecan pie with a cup of good strong coffee. Lillian used to make a cup of coffee you could stand a spoon in, not like the brown water they serve in here.

SARAH: Lillian was your —

HANK: First wife. She was the sweet to my bitter, I suppose.

SARAH: Is she —

HANK: Alive? Dunno. Not much reason to talk after a divorce with no kids.

SARAH: But your son —

HANK: Ahh, him. Different wife. Clara. She's dead.

SARAH: Oh.

HANK: She was a horrible cook.

SARAH: You must miss her.

HANK: Not her cooking . . . she was a good girl.

[*Beat*]

Why're you asking me this? They can't cook any of those things here. Everything has to be easy to chew. This coming from Kathleen? She planning something?

SARAH: No.

HANK: This have to do with my birthday?

SARAH: I don't know what they have planned for your birthday.

HANK: Cause I don't want a party.

SARAH: You don't want to do something fun?

HANK: I don't want a party. You hear me? I don't want it!

SARAH: Okay.

HANK: I don't want it.

[*Silence*]

SARAH: Why'd you run off?

HANK: What?

SARAH: When they found you in the field. Why'd you run off?

HANK: I can't remember.

SARAH: Did you get bored?

HANK: I'm old. I can't remember.

SARAH: Where were you going?

[*HANK thinks and shrugs.*]

HANK: Well, it got me here, into a room of my own. I was sharing with Reggie, but lockdown means your own space.

SARAH: So you did it on purpose?

HANK: No.

SARAH: Then why put yourself in danger?

HANK: I really can't remember. There was something, something I had to see.

SARAH: What?

HANK: It was urgent. If only I could remember. [*Tries to remember*] nope . . . gone.

SARAH: Maybe it'll come back to you.

HANK: Doubt it.

SCENE 5

KATHLEEN sits drinking tea at her desk. SARAH enters.

KATHLEEN: How'd it go?

SARAH: Fine, I guess.

KATHLEEN: Peppermint tea?

[*SARAH opens her mouth to show a mint.*]

SARAH: No thanks. I got a candy from Hank's room.

[*SARAH rubs her forehead.*]

Have you got an aspirin?

[*KATHLEEN opens a drawer.*]

KATHLEEN: Aspirin or ibuprofen?
SARAH: Doesn't matter.

[*SARAH swallows the pills. KATHLEEN pours herself a cup of tea.*]

KATHLEEN: What do you think we should serve for Hank's birthday?
SARAH: I don't think a party is such a good idea.
KATHLEEN: How can we let a man that has lived a hundred years go uncelebrated?
SARAH: He doesn't want anything like that.
KATHLEEN: Sometimes people aren't sure about what they want.

[*SARAH gives KATHLEEN a look.*]

SARAH: He's pretty sure. He's pretty sure about most things.
KATHLEEN: Hank wasn't sure he wanted to come here, but after his wife, Mona, died, Hank was all alone in their condo. After about three months, a man came to the door looking for odd jobs, cutting grass, that sort of thing. There was a picture on the wall of Hank in full uniform and the man asked about it. Hank said that he was a proud veteran and perfectly able to cut his

own lawn. The next week, a man showed up on his door asking for money for war orphans. Hank didn't recognize him as the man who offered to cut his grass. While Hank wrote a cheque for three hundred dollars, the man looked at the picture on the wall and asked how he, a man who had seen active service, could give so little. Ashamed, Hank added a zero. When Hank's son Neil went over his taxes, he found that over ten thousand dollars had gone out to bogus charities. Hank doesn't look like it, but he needs help. We can help.

SARAH: But a party isn't really his style.

KATHLEEN: Sarah, before working here, how much time had you spent in a nursing home?

SARAH: My grandmother was in a nursing home before she died.

KATHLEEN: And how many times did you visit her?

SARAH: Twice . . . once.

KATHLEEN: Over a month?

SARAH: Over three years.

KATHLEEN: It's our job to celebrate.

[*Beat*]

SARAH: Okay, but no hors d'oeuvres.

SCENE 6

SARAH enters HANK's empty room. She has a plastic bag containing a bottle of glue and carries two cups of coffee. HANK can be heard yelling down the hall.

HANK: You can't do this! Are we in a prison? I won't stop yelling! I won't stop yelling until someone listens to me! You have no right!

[*HANK enters the room and sees SARAH.*]

Was it you?

SARAH: What?

HANK: Was it you who told on me?

SARAH: I don't know what you're talking about.

HANK: She's taken my mints! My Scottish mints! They've been confiscated. They're a choking hazard.

SARAH: It wasn't me . . . I had one when I left your . . . [*realizing*] oh, I had one when I left your room the other day . . . and spoke with Kathleen.

HANK: Traitor!

SARAH: I didn't tell on you. I just told her that I got a candy — it never occurred to me.

HANK: She searched my room as if I'm a criminal.

SARAH: I had no idea it would be a problem.

HANK: Of course it's a problem. Everything here is a problem. Everything that adds a shred of pleasure, a shred of dignity is a problem. She had no right to take them!

SARAH: I brought you a cup of coffee.

HANK: They were mine, in my room. They were no one else's business.

SARAH: Here, dark roast. As bitter as I could get it.

[*HANK fumes.*]

HANK: No one else's business.

SARAH: Please? You know it's better than the stuff they have here.

[*HANK silently takes the coffee and drinks.*]

I got some glue. Maybe we can start the model today?

[*Silence.*]

[*SARAH gets up and takes the model out of the closet. She opens the glue and looks at the pieces. She lays them out on the table. After assessing the parts, she takes two and starts to put them together. HANK watches her.*]

HANK: You're doing it wrong.

SARAH: Isn't this part of the propeller?

HANK: No, it goes over the gun turret.

[*HANK takes the piece and shows her.*]

SARAH: Oh, [*picking up a piece*] what's this thing?

HANK: The bomb doors. Those opened like this during the bomb run. Your guts open to the world, a quarter inch of metal keeping you in and the night out.

[*Beat*]

This is good coffee.

SARAH: You're welcome.

HANK: Thank you.

SARAH: You know, Kathleen's just trying to keep you safe.

HANK: I don't want safe. What's the point of safe? I flew twenty-four missions in the pitch dark and never stopped because it was unsafe. I'd take the cold metal of a fuselage over these sterile walls any day.

SARAH: You fly this thing all by yourself?

HANK: Crew of seven. Wireless operator, mid gunner, bomb aimer, flight engineer, navigator, and the pilot.

SARAH: That's six.

HANK: Tail gunner. Seven . . . I saw some things with those boys.

SARAH: Same crew?

HANK: Twenty-four missions.

SARAH: Did you keep in touch after the war?

HANK: They're all dead now.

SARAH: I'm sorry.

HANK: Don't say that. People die. All the time. Here, they try and keep it pretty quiet. They don't want to spook the biddies with just how many people are scraped off the floor in a week, but I know. The EMS practically have their own parking spot out front. I've been in that ambulance five times. Broken down into parts, a prostate, a back, a hip, lungs, and a heart. They can manage each, but they can't cure old age. Wish they'd stop trying.

SARAH: Hank, sit down. You're getting agitated.

HANK: Reggie wasn't in his chair last night.

SARAH: What chair?

HANK: In the dining room. It was empty.

SARAH: Oh?

HANK: Yesterday was Thursday.

SARAH: Right . . .

HANK: They serve borscht on Thursdays.

SARAH: Every Thursday.

HANK: Every Thursday.

SARAH: Maybe he didn't want any.

HANK: He loves beets. Never passes up a bowl of 'em. I know cause it's the same.

SARAH: What's the same?

HANK: The chairs. You come in to eat your fresh egg after a long night. Nobody talks about it, but you notice. The empty chairs . . . all those boys who won't get their egg.

[*HANK tries to get the pieces of the model together.*]

SARAH: Let's take a break. You look tired.

HANK: I'm tired of it all. People die in here, and no one wants to talk about it.

SARAH: You're not dying. You're going to turn one hundred.

HANK: That's not my accomplishment. It's the doctor's, it's Kathleen's . . . it's yours. I wish you'd just let me go.

SARAH: Did you sleep last night?

HANK: I can't sleep in here. I can't sleep, and they won't let me out. I'm trapped in here all night. It's at night that I can feel it.

[*HANK gets up and grabs his walker.*]

SARAH: Hank, why don't you lie down? Just for a little while.

HANK: I just need to get outside.

SARAH: You've had a rough day, and you're upset.

[*She looks through his pill bottles.*]

Did they give you your medication?

HANK: I can't remember. I'm losing my memory, my glasses, my friends . . .

SARAH: Shhh

[*She gently leads him back to bed.*]

HANK: I'm tired of losing things.

SARAH: It's okay. Just a little sleep.

[*Beat*]

I'm sorry about your mints.

HANK: Again with the sorry, don't say sorry.

SARAH: Maybe I can get them back.

HANK: Once something is taken away, it's gone . . . for good.

[*She tucks him in bed.*]

SARAH: Things will be better after a rest.

[*Once he is settled, she walks to the door.*]

HANK: Sarah?

[*SARAH looks back.*]

SARAH: Yes, Hank?

HANK: No one asked me if this is what I wanted.

[*SARAH closes HANK's door and stands, taking a moment to breathe in what just happened. She lifts her hands to see that they are shaking. KATHLEEN walks by.*]

KATHLEEN: Sarah?

SARAH: [*tucking her hands behind her back*] What?

KATHLEEN: You okay?

SARAH: Yeah, just a little dizzy. Sorry.

KATHLEEN: How late are you scheduled?

SARAH: I'm off at five.

KATHLEEN: Could you stay tonight? I sent Sophie home with a cold, and we're already tight for staff.

SARAH: I have an appointment . . . but I could cancel it.

KATHLEEN: That would be great.

SARAH: Sure. Yeah, no problem. No problem at all.

[*KATHLEEN leaves. SARAH takes out her phone and dials a number.*]

Hello? This is Sarah Baker. I'm not going to be able to make my appointment today with Dr. Illich.

[*SARAH takes out a bottle of aspirin and takes two pills.*]

SCENE 7

KATHLEEN and SARAH sit at the desk. KATHLEEN reads magazines and pamphlets, getting ideas for the party. She looks at her watch.

KATHLEEN: I've got ten minutes until I need to check on Rosalie before she goes to bed.

[*She hands SARAH a list.*]

Here's the list of people to invite to Hank's birthday party.

[*SARAH reads through the list.*]

SARAH: Sonny Smith? From the news?

KATHLEEN: The news loves feel-good stories like this one.

SARAH: He's the weather guy.

KATHLEEN: They like to put a story like this in between politics and the weekend forecast. Makes a rainy Saturday easier to take.

SARAH: You think Hank's son will come?

KATHLEEN: [*shrugs*] He'll get an invitation.

[*She continues to read the list. KATHLEEN relaxes.*]

Tea?

SARAH: Do we have any coffee?

KATHLEEN: There might be some in the staff room. It's from this morning.

SARAH: I'll have a cup of tea.

[*KATHLEEN pours SARAH a cup of tea.*]

KATHLEEN: It's Earl Grey.

SARAH: Good. I need the caffeine.

KATHLEEN: Those invites need to go out this week.

SARAH: I'll get them out tomorrow.

KATHLEEN: Perfect.

[*Beat*]

SARAH: Um, can you give Hank his mints back?

KATHLEEN: I can't. It's against policy.

SARAH: If he wants to have some peppermints beside his bed, he should be able to do that.

KATHLEEN: The residents need to eat in the dining room where we can keep an eye on them.

SARAH: He likes to eat them while watching television.

KATHLEEN: I don't have the staff needed to supervise each room at all times.

SARAH: Can't we let the man have the few bits of independence he has left?

KATHLEEN: It's dangerous.

SARAH: Just this once. His best friend just died.

KATHLEEN: What?

SARAH: Reggie wasn't at dinner last night.

KATHLEEN: . . . No.

SARAH: And it was Thursday.

KATHLEEN: His niece is here on a business trip from Halifax. She took him out for the afternoon, and they decided to go out for dinner.

SARAH: I thought he never missed —

KATHLEEN: And Reggie is not Hank's best friend.

SARAH: Oh.

[*KATHLEEN flips through a pamphlet.*]

KATHLEEN: I think they went to the Keg.

[*Beat. KATHLEEN reads the pamphlet.*]

What do you think about a band? For the party? I was thinking a band, you know with horns that can play all that old-timey stuff.

SARAH: A big band.

KATHLEEN: Yes, a big band . . . but smaller. [*She looks at the pamphlet*] It's not cheap.

SARAH: A small band.

KATHLEEN: A small big band.

SARAH: Gotcha.

KATHLEEN: And the cake . . . We usually order from Crusty's for cakes. They can do a sugar-free chocolate or vanilla.

SARAH: What about pecan pie?

KATHLEEN: We have to think of the diabetics.

[*KATHLEEN flips through pictures of cake. SARAH joins in the search. HANK comes shuffling out of his room in a trance-like state.*]

SARAH: [*getting up to go see him*] Hank?

[*KATHLEEN catches her by the wrist.*]

KATHLEEN: You'll frighten him.

SARAH: What's he doing?

KATHLEEN: He's sundowning.

SARAH: What's that?

KATHLEEN: Sundowning. If you interrupt him, he'll get confused and frightened. Don't upset him.

[*Mumbling as she searches*] Bakeries . . .

[*HANK wanders to the front door. He slowly tries to open the door.*]

Have you ever had the olive cheese bread from Milano's? Amazing.

[*She looks up to see SARAH watching HANK.*]

It's a symptom of dementia that only seems to happen as the sun sets. Sometimes they yell, sometimes they fight, and some sit and shake. Hank just wanders to the front door.

SARAH: He's trying to get out.

KATHLEEN: It's okay. The doors are locked.

[*Searches through her materials*]

Pies . . . I wonder if they'd do a sugar free option.

SARAH: Where's he trying to get to?

KATHLEEN: Who knows?

[*KATHLEEN pours herself another cup of tea as they watch.*]

Some say it's the fading light. As the shadows get longer, they could be a trigger. Some think it's not enough exercise, others think too much exercise. Nobody knows for sure why it happens.

[*Unable to open the door, HANK turns around and heads back to his room.*]

He didn't have any coffee this afternoon, did he?

SARAH: Is that what did it?

KATHLEEN: Could be.

SARAH: A grande Americano.

KATHLEEN: An Americano.

SARAH: A grande . . . I wanted him to have a treat.

KATHLEEN: Look Sarah, you care. I'm glad you care, but you are taking care of one person. I have sixty to see through each day and night. Things have to be run a certain way to make sure everyone is taken care of. I've been doing this for a long time, and I'm doing the very best I can with the resources I've got.

[*KATHLEEN's pager goes off.*]

That's Rosalie. I have to go.

[*KATHLEEN leaves.*]

SARAH: Sorry.

[*SARAH gets up and walks to the door that HANK had been trying to open. She tries opening it, but can't. She looks through the window, up at the night sky.*]

SCENE 8

HANK and SARAH sit, gluing the model together in HANK's room. The model is two-thirds done.

SARAH: You know there are a lot of women at the lodge. Maybe you'd like to meet someone.

HANK: Let's not make this one of those things. Just because there's a man and a woman — and we're still breathing, despite the sleep apnea — we should become an item? Let's not go down that cliché road.

SARAH: You said you miss adventure, risk taking, well, there's no bigger risk than romance.

HANK: I'm not slow dancing with a hip replacement so you and Kathleen have something to giggle about while having your tea.

SARAH: I think you're just being shy.

HANK: Listen, you won't understand this, but a young man is completely led by his —

SARAH: Gonads. I've heard.

HANK: You've heard, but you can't understand how much it rules you. When we were naming our Lanc we couldn't agree on anything. The name was of utmost importance. Had to be something we could all get behind . . . something that spoke to seven boys from across Canada. Had to be something that reminded us why we were there.

SARAH: So? What was the decision?

HANK: 'Mollie's Legs.' We knew we had to get home to see Mollie's Legs.

SARAH: Who's Mollie?

HANK: We all had a Mollie back home. I've had three wives. It was only after my eighty-fifth birthday that I began to think with the right head. Just let me enjoy this new clarity of thought.

SARAH: I just think —

HANK: What about you?

SARAH: What about me?

HANK: You must have a life outside of this place.

SARAH: I do. I do. Of course, I do.

[*Beat*]

I have school.

HANK: That's not what I mean. I mean the thing that you want to get back home to.

SARAH: Do I have a boyfriend?

HANK: If that's what you want to talk about.

SARAH: I don't . . . and I did. We broke up two years ago.

HANK: Two years ago?

SARAH: When things fell apart.

HANK: I never learned how to keep things together either.

SARAH: I like being alone. Pass the glue.

HANK: You must have friends.

SARAH: I have friends. I don't have time for them right now. This program keeps me pretty busy. I have a cat.

HANK: You sound like my son. Everyone's so busy. Everyone's too busy.

SARAH: I am busy.

HANK: You're not that busy.

SARAH: I have two jobs. I work here and at the E.R.

HANK: So?

SARAH: And I have homework.

HANK: You're still not that busy.

SARAH: I am. I'm busy. My friends understand.

HANK: Make time for them. You have more time than you think when you're young, but it goes fast and then goes on too long. Glue.

SARAH: People are busy. Your son is probably busy.

HANK: He is.

SARAH: I'm sure he's just got a lot going on.

[*HANK nods.*]

HANK: Grandkids.

SARAH: And work.

HANK: He's consulting now that he's retired.

SARAH: Is he married?

HANK: Nice woman. She's going through breast cancer treatments.

SARAH: How is she?

HANK: Doing well.

SARAH: I'm sure he'd come if he had more time.

HANK: He wouldn't.

SARAH: It doesn't mean he's not thinking about you.

HANK: He doesn't have to. I'm fed and watered. He doesn't have to worry.

SARAH: Everyone's just so busy.

HANK: Except me.

[*Beat*]

[*SARAH picks up a piece of the model, she picks up the glue and drops it.*]

SARAH: Sorry.

HANK: Don't say that.

[*SARAH tries to pick up the glue, and it falls again.*]

Don't say it.

[*SARAH lifts her hands and watches them shake.*]

HANK: Sarah, what's wrong?

SARAH: Nothing. Please? Nothing's wrong. I'm fine. Let's just finish the wing.

[*SARAH goes to pick up the wing, but drops it.*]

Sorry. Sorry. It'll go away. I'm just tired.

[*She looks at him.*]

Are you tired? Did you sleep? You never sleep.

HANK: I'm fine.

SARAH: Me too. I'm fine. I did a double shift.

[*She picks up the wing and drops it.*]

I can fix it.

[*HANK takes her hands into his own. She looks at him, terrified.*]

Please don't tell.

HANK: You had too much coffee.

SARAH: Can we just finish the wing?

[*HANK takes the wing and manages to put it together.*]

HANK: There.

SARAH: Thank you.

SCENE 9

HANK and KATHLEEN are overheard sparring in the bathroom.

KATHLEEN: Let me help.

HANK: I can do it just fine on my own.

[Beat]

I can't go with you watching me.

KATHLEEN: Then just let me help —

HANK: No!

KATHLEEN: Please —

HANK: I said no.

KATHLEEN: Then I have no choice to but to watch.

HANK: Go away!

KATHLEEN: I don't enjoy it, either.

HANK: I said go away!

KATHLEEN: Please, it's just easier if you sit down.

HANK: I can stand on my own two feet like any other man.

KATHLEEN: Hank, it just keeps you from becoming unsteady.

HANK: I'm not gonna sit down to pee!

KATHLEEN: Fine!

[KATHLEEN exits the bathroom and finds SARAH entering HANK's room.]

SARAH: What's going on?

KATHLEEN: He's been like this all morning.

HANK: *[from the bathroom]* I can still hear you!

[*The toilet flushes.*]

KATHLEEN: [*To HANK*] You can tell the cleaning staff your decision!

[*HANK enters from the bathroom.*]

HANK: Sarah?

SARAH: Hi, Hank.

KATHLEEN: Maybe you can talk to him.

[*KATHLEEN leaves, frustrated.*]

HANK: It's your day off.

SARAH: I just thought I'd stop in and see how you're doing.

HANK: I'm fine.

SARAH: Good, me too. Maybe we could get some of the model finished. We're so close.

[*She settles, and starts to lay out the pieces of the model.*]

Pass the glue. Let's get started.

[*HANK passes her the glue from where it sits on the shelf.*]

HANK: Are you okay?

SARAH: Me? I'm fine.

HANK: You're acting as nervous as a nun in a cucumber field.

SARAH: What was Kathleen so upset about?

HANK: Nothing. It's nothing.

[*Beat*]

44

No one comes here when they don't have to.

SARAH: I was in the neighbourhood.

HANK: In the neighbourhood?

SARAH: Yup.

[SARAH starts in on the model. She notices that HANK is watching her.]

Fine. I wanted to give you something.

[She pulls a bag out of her purse and plops it in HANK's lap.]

Open it.

HANK: What is it?

SARAH: Open it! It's a birthday present.

HANK: It's not my birthday till Saturday.

SARAH: Open it.

[HANK stares at her.]

Fine.

[SARAH opens it herself, revealing a bag of scotch mints.]

Ta-da! Scotch mints! A truly dignified candy!

HANK: Sarah, where were you this morning?

SARAH: I got them back for you. I got them back. Have you got a bowl I could put these in? [She turns to the closet] There must be something in here.

[She finds the box with the rabbit's foot in it.]

Perfect.

[*She opens the box and lifts out the rabbit's foot.* HANK *puts out his hand and she gives it to him. She fills the box with mints.*]

Happy birthday!

[*Beat*]

HANK: It's not my birthday.
SARAH: Fine.

[*She pops a mint in her mouth.*]

Delicious.

HANK: Where were you this morning?
SARAH: What do you mean?
HANK: You said you were in the neighbourhood. Where were you?
SARAH: I might've popped in at the doctor's on the way.
HANK: What did he say?
SARAH: Nothing.
HANK: Nothing?
SARAH: Nothing I didn't already know.

[SARAH *eats another mint.*]

You shouldn't be such a grump about your birthday. People are just trying to be nice to you.

HANK: Are you okay?
SARAH: I told you, I'm fine.
HANK: Did the doctor say you'll be okay?

[*SARAH glues the model together.*]

SARAH: Look at this clunky old thing. How'd it ever get off the ground?

[*Beat. HANK waits.*]

He doesn't know. Nobody knows. There's not much good I can do at home, so I came here. Might as well make myself useful.

[*She picks up the model.*]

How'd they get it to fly?

HANK: Took four Merlin engines to get it up over the water and into enemy territory. To make it lighter, they took out all the armour except for a scrap they left behind the pilot's head.

[*Beat*]

Sarah?

SARAH: Do I look sick?

HANK: No.

SARAH: I don't feel sick.

HANK: Are you?

[*She plays with the model.*]

SARAH: They took out all the armour and you still got in that plane? You knew what could happen every time you got in that plane . . . and you did it anyway.

[*She looks at him.*]

47

Oh, It's not like that. It's not cancer or anything. It's a good disease . . . if you've got to have one. MS . . . multiple sclerosis.

HANK: When did this happen?

SARAH: Oh, it's not new. I've known since Jonah and I lived together, my first year of nursing. I'm used to it. The doctor just wanted to talk.

HANK: What did he say?

SARAH: He went over my MRI. Told me we could try another medication, see if that slows it down.

[*Beat*]

HANK: Multiple sclerosis.

SARAH: Multiple multiple sclerosis . . . thirty-one new lesions on my brain. Pass me the glue.

[*HANK hands her the glue. She picks up the model and starts going to work.*]

[*Beat*]

Did you always want to fly?

HANK: Most young men have some kind of romance with the air. We all thought we'd be pilots. Never figured I'd end up being an arse-end Charlie. Nobody wants to be a rear tail gunner . . . no one. Most of 'em died up there alone in the tail.

SARAH: But you didn't.

HANK: I didn't.

SARAH: Maybe it was your rabbit's foot.

HANK: Maybe.

SARAH: Do you miss it?

HANK: Miss it more than my wives.

SARAH: You must have been glad when it was over.

HANK: We were all glad when the war was over. It was a terrible conflict. You can be glad something is over and still miss it. I feel the same way about my marriages.

SARAH: What got you through those missions?

HANK: It's strange, but I think the cold got me through. They gave us heated suits, but they didn't always work. The cold was something to concentrate on . . . you couldn't let your mind wander. The second you got in that tin can, you were in for seven hours. All you had was the sound of the engines and darkness. It was like being tossed into a swimming hole. You didn't know what was lurking around you, where it would come from. It's all flying in the dark hoping you won't get hit.

SARAH: How'd you make yourself do it?

HANK: There wasn't a choice.

[*Beat*]

SARAH: No. There isn't.

[*SARAH glues the pieces of plane together.*]

I saw a lady in the E.R. She couldn't walk, her husband had to lift her out of her wheelchair and into bed each night. I thought if I did all the right things. Ate healthy food. Sleep more than five hours. Do well at school. I drink too much coffee. Coffee's not good for me.

HANK: Have you got someone to talk to?

SARAH: I don't want to talk to anyone.

HANK: It might make you feel better.

SARAH: Did you talk to your crew?

HANK: No one said much during those seven hours — only to deliver a message: change of course, aircraft sighting — I guess I coulda warmed up a bit in the fuselage, gotten some tea off Vic's thermos, but the clouds might break, and I needed to be ready. I was alone back there, but I knew they were there.

SARAH: You ever get hit?

HANK: Almost. It was our twenty-fourth mission. We knew we were flying against the odds. That night seemed like a milk run, 'cept we got coned in the searchlights on the way back. We started to take a lot of flak. It wasn't until we got back on the ground that my hands started to shake. Somebody handed me a cup of coffee with a stiff shot of rum in it, told me to drink it before we got in the debriefing room. One of the officers musta noticed the shaking, cause they grounded me for two weeks while the doctors looked me over to see if . . . to see, I only ever saw it once . . . in a parade square, a navigator I think, stripped of his wings and rank badges. LMF, Lack of Moral Fibre. I remember him standing in the middle of the square, head down while he picked at the strands of thread where his stripes used to be. I pushed it down until the shaking stopped. Till they said I was okay.

SARAH: It's better if people think you're okay, because than you don't have to worry about them worrying about you.

HANK: Clara used to worry about me all the time. Used to drive me up the wall. Did I eat enough? Did I sleep enough? I just wanted her to leave me alone.

SARAH: Exactly.

HANK: And now I am.

[*Beat*]

SARAH: Are you going to tell me to be grateful?

HANK: No.

SARAH: Because I have people who love me?

HANK: So did I. I still left.

SARAH: Why?

HANK: Because they needed me to be okay. And I hated them for it.

SARAH: When I told my Mum I was sick, she cried. My Dad said he would pray for me. I didn't know what to do, so I hung up the phone and went to work. Jonah kept asking me to talk about it. Said I should see a psychologist. I didn't have time. There were people in the E.R. who needed help, I didn't. I think he hated that I didn't fall apart. I moved out three weeks later. I'm fine with it. They say everything happens for a reason.

HANK: They are lying. Somebody took my place while the doctors looked me over. Every time my crew went up, I'd wait for the sound of the engines returning. One night, I heard the Lancs coming in, some roaring, some limping. Smoke billowing in the air — it had been a rough night. I walked up the steps to the control tower. More planes hobbled on to the tarmac. I asked, "Mollie's Legs?"

"Not yet."

I waited. It was cold. I was in my pajamas.

"Mollie's Legs?"

"Still no sight."

I stood and stared at the sky, the night was starting to bleed with light. I waited, shivering. Finally, one of the ground crew walked down the steps. They were done for the night. I remember he put a hand on my shoulder and said, "sorry."

Sorry? Can you get more Canadian? Sorry. I hate that word. I'll never forget standing under that sky, waiting, . . . it just seemed to go on forever.

SARAH: I don't want to be treated like a sick person.

HANK: I don't want to be treated like an old person.

[*Beat*]

Maybe some made their peace, but England had as many bars as churches . . . so I never had to. When Neil was growing up, I wasn't around much, and even when I was, I wasn't there — I got stuck. I was back in a field looking at the sky.

SARAH: That's why you go out in the middle of the night.

HANK: Maybe.

SARAH: You're waiting for your plane to come in.

HANK: But it never comes.

SCENE 10

KATHLEEN sits blowing up balloons at her desk. She tries to fit them in a garbage bag. SARAH enters carrying pecan pies from the bakery.

KATHLEEN: Great! Thank you.

SARAH: Anything else?

KATHLEEN: Let me just check the list.

[*She pulls out the list and reads.*]

Band?

SARAH: Check. We'll set up tomorrow morning.

KATHLEEN: Cake?

SARAH: And pecan pie. Check.

KATHLEEN: Decorations?

SARAH: [*Gestures to the balloons*] Check.

KATHLEEN: Is the weatherman coming?

SARAH: He wants to do a live interview.

KATHLEEN: Fantastic.

SARAH: Is Hank's son coming?

KATHLEEN: Haven't heard back.

SARAH: His wife is sick.

KATHLEEN: He's busy.

SARAH: Yeah.

[*KATHLEEN doublechecks her list.*]

KATHLEEN: Well, I actually think we're ready.

SARAH: Ready as we'll ever be.

KATHLEEN: This is going to be a wonderful surprise party.

SARAH: It certainly will be a surprise.

SCENE 11

Nighttime. SARAH gently enters HANK's room. The finished model sits on the bedside table.

SARAH: Are you awake?

HANK: I'm always awake.

SARAH: I brought you something.

[*SARAH gives HANK an envelope.*]

Don't worry. It's not a birthday present.

HANK: What is it?

SARAH: Open it.

[*HANK reaches into the envelope. He pulls out the decals.*]

I wasn't sure about the colours. I tried to get it as close as I could.

HANK: Mollie's Legs. Where did you find these?

SARAH: I thought maybe we could finish your plane.

[*SARAH passes HANK the model plane. She pulls off a decal and gives it to HANK. He puts it on the plane. He looks at it, taking it in.*]

HANK: Bernie on wireless; Fred, mid gunner; Bert, bomb aimer; Sandy, flight engineer; Trevor, navigator; and the pilot, Vic.

[*HANK holds up the plane.*]

SARAH: And you.

HANK: Tail gunner.

[*He holds it up.*]

There she is.

SARAH: Do you like it?

HANK: I wish the boys could see her.

SARAH: Let's show them.

HANK: What do you mean?

SARAH: Let's see what she looks like in the night sky.

HANK: The door's locked.

[*SARAH holds up a key card.*]

SARAH: I could use some fresh air.

[*She helps* HANK *up and to his walker. She carries the plane.*]

HANK: Where are we going?

SARAH: No more waiting.

[*They arrive at a quiet spot in the field.* HANK *looks up at the sky.*]

What was it like flying into battle?

HANK: Cold.

SARAH: Were you scared?

HANK: Some of the guys said they weren't, but I was.

SARAH: Me too.

HANK: It's funny we believe in justice so deeply. We think there is a straight line between cause and effect, right and wrong, but there is another world that holds this tiny belief in its hands, ready to crumple it at will. Truth is, there is no reason, there is no logic. There's no reason those boys were shot out of the sky and nothing about me standing here . . . or you . . . or any of it is fair. It's all just flying in the dark, hoping you won't get hit.

[HANK *lifts up the plane.*]

Per Ardua Ad Astra. The motto of the Royal Canadian Air Force.

SARAH: What's it mean?

HANK: Through adversity to the stars.

[HANK *lifts the plane high to see it against the sky.*]

Bert from Saskatoon, Bernie from Vancouver, Sandy from Medicine Hat, Fred from Antigonish, Trevor from Strathmore, and Vic from Kamloops . . . we did see some stars. Didn't we boys? We did see some stars.

[*He lays the plane on the ground, turns, and walks towards* SARAH, *passing her as he heads back towards the lodge.* SARAH *looks up at the sky before following him back.*]

SCENE 12

Back at the lodge

HANK: I'm tired.

[SARAH *looks at her watch.*]

SARAH: It's after midnight.

HANK: Is it?

SARAH: Happy birthday.

HANK: Thank you.

SARAH: I should warn you. There's going to be a party for you. Kathleen's been planning it for weeks. You think you can bear it?

HANK: I've been through worse.

[*HANK yawns.*]

SARAH: You're tired.

HANK: I'm old.

SARAH: Let's get you ready for bed.

HANK: No fussing. I'll be fine on my own. Would you get me something out of the closet?

SARAH: Sure.

HANK: It's in a black bag at the back.

[*SARAH rifles through the closet and pulls out a black garment bag.*]

Just lay it out. I'll wear it to the party.

[*SARAH lays the garment bag on the bed.*]

SARAH: Well, being here with you, it does feel like we met for a reason.

HANK: No reason. Just pure dumb luck.

SARAH: I'll take it.

HANK: It's all we've got.

[*SARAH kisses his cheek.*]

You're a good girl.

SARAH: Happy birthday Hank.

[*She picks up her purse.*]

HANK: Sarah?

SARAH: Yes?

HANK: Don't spend the rest of your days alone in a field.

SARAH: [*She nods*] . . . Have a good sleep, Hank.

HANK: I think I will.

SARAH: I'll see you tomorrow at the party.

[*SARAH leaves. Once she is gone, HANK gets up and opens the garment bag. He pulls out his Royal Canadian Air Force uniform. He puts on his coat and hat. He checks himself over in the mirror. He pulls out a piece of paper and writes a small note. He*] *rummages in the closet, finds a small box, and puts it on top of the note. He crawls into bed wearing his uniform.*]

HANK: No more waiting.

SCENE 13

SARAH walks into the lodge with a bundle of balloons and a bouquet of flowers.

SARAH: Happy birthday! Hank?

[*KATHLEEN enters following SARAH.*]

Today's the day! Big crowd out there!

[*SARAH turns around to see KATHLEEN.*]

Where's the birthday boy?

KATHLEEN: Sarah?

SARAH: Guess who I just met in the parking lot? Neil's here . . . He made it . . . and his grandkids too! Where's Hank? I've gotta see this.

KATHLEEN: Sarah, wait.

SARAH: Where is he?

KATHLEEN: Sarah, Hank's gone.

SARAH: Did you check the field?

KATHLEEN: No.

SARAH: He probably saw the hors d'oeuvres in the hallway. I'll find him and talk to him. He'll be fine.

KATHLEEN: Sarah, Hank died last night.

SARAH: I just saw him.

KATHLEEN: Peacefully in his sleep.

SARAH: Hank never slept.

KATHLEEN: Sarah . . .

SARAH: I just took him out yesterday. He said he was tired. I didn't, I'm sorry, Kathleen.

KATHLEEN: Sarah, he was one hundred years old.

SARAH: He could have been here. He could have been here, but I, I'm so sorry.

KATHLEEN: Don't be sorry. He was ready. He wouldn't want you to be sorry, would he?

SARAH: No.

KATHLEEN: Be sad . . . but don't be sorry.

[*Beat*]

SARAH: Who's with the residents?

KATHLEEN: Rosalie is going to do a live weather report with Sonny. Sophie's dishing out the pie. No point in wasting it.

SARAH: Shouldn't we be there?

KATHLEEN: In a minute.

[*KATHLEEN hands SARAH the small box and note.*]

This was on the table.

SARAH: What is it?

KATHLEEN: It has your name on it.

[*SARAH opens the note and reads.*]

SARAH: "Through adversity to the stars."

[*She opens the box and pulls out the rabbit's foot.*]

[*She is hit by grief.*]

[*After a few moments* SARAH *sits up, trying to compose herself.*]

Kathleen, if I take a few days off . . . can I come back?
KATHLEEN: You want to come back here?
SARAH: Please.
KATHLEEN: Of course you can. You take the time you need.
SARAH: Thank you.

[*They sit, feeling the loss of* HANK. *She and* KATHLEEN *look at each other and around the room.*]

KATHLEEN: What a god-awful colour. What is that?

[*SARAH takes in the room.*]

SARAH: Puce.

The end.

CANADIANS IN BOMBER COMMAND, AGING IN THE AFTERMATH OF WAR, AND THE STAGING OF *FLIGHT RISK*

Flying in the Dark: The Canadian Bomber Command Experience and Meg Braem's *Flight Risk*

William John Pratt

We are all flying in the dark. As much as we try to navigate a safe and satisfying course, at any moment our luck can turn; we find dear friends departing, health collapsing, our burning craft hurtling to earth. Death is as certain as gravity, yet we clench our eyes shut and hope for another mission before the end. Not everything happens for a reason. Some things just happen. You lose your friends. You lose your health. You lose your dignity. We don't really get to control how things go. Trapped in a risky situation, it is easy to be paralyzed by fear or grief, feeling caught by the searchlights and powerless to evade the inevitable. When your number's up, optimism is denial. It might be a coping mechanism, but so is acceptance. We might as well just open our eyes and peer out into the darkness, try to identify enemy fighters approaching, our murky anxieties and bodily frailties. During the Second World War, bomber aircrew faced the fates and furies alongside their band of brothers, men whose aptitudes and abilities meant life or death for them all. They knew the odds were stacked against them, but they grimaced and held on for the ride. We can all hope to have a few companions on our own flights. Fellow riders might break our fearful grip, call for evasive maneuvers, or just commiserate about the inevitable. Meg Braem's play suggests life's companions, our own fellow aircrew, can come in unexpected forms.

In the opening lines of *Flight Risk,* the cantankerous ninety-nine-year-old veteran Henry Dunfield informs his new nurse that he's been "Hank since the war." As the play continues, we find that the global conflict was transformative for this veteran of Bomber Command. The former tail gunner has troubling memories of the war; he grieves fellow aircrew of his Lancaster bomber who never made it back from their fatal mission. The war was liminal and indelible; it formed a violent coming of age. Bomber motifs of risk, searching, and chance structure Hank's considerations of his own mortality and form a stark contrast to the banal grind of institutionalized aging. These wartime metaphors also shape his initial resistance to, and then counselling of, the busy young nurse who tries her best to ignore her own fragile humanity. Aircrew memoirs grant us a glimpse into the world of Canadian bomber aircrew in the Second World War. Their authors' reminiscences of coping with loss, chance, and mortality seem apt for understanding our own adversities, even if we can, perhaps, never know exactly what it felt like for the young men to take to the skies in a struggle of life and death.

The British Royal Air Force (RAF) formed Bomber Command in the interwar years as a separate organization to harness the potential of the bomber. During the First World War, bombers grew in their capacity to carry explosive devastation to the enemy, and after 1918 theorists continued to develop military doctrine surrounding these deadly tools. By the time that Hitler's Wehrmacht invaded Poland in September 1939 and the Second World War in Europe began, nations like Germany and Britain had invested considerable resources in building up their bomber fleets. Interwar bombing doctrine in various countries dreamed of great potential for the technology: bombers could pinpoint critical industries or infrastructure, or even erode morale to such an extent that enemy states would collapse. The Germans proved the devastating potential of the modern bomber in 1937, when (alongside fascist Italy's air force) the bombing of Guernica during the Spanish Civil War drew international headlines, including "Mass Murder in Guernica" from the *New York Times* and the tagline "Bodies Lie in Heaps," from Toronto's *Globe and Mail*.[1] The machines would only grow more capable, and the twin-engine bombers that started the war were soon eclipsed by four-engine heavy bombers like the Lancaster. Despite the impressive abilities of mid-war bombers in lifting some fourteen thousand pounds of explosives up to eighteen thousand feet and higher, Allied bombers were found too vulnerable to attack German air defences in broad daylight. Instead, Bomber Command took to night raids for most of the war, where difficulties in targeting and navigation abounded. This, in turn, led to a preference in the minds of RAF leaders such as Commander-in-Chief Bomber Command, Arthur 'Bomber' Harris, for the area bombing of industrial areas and cities (which were much easier to find and hit at night than specific industrial installations), and consequently to tragic losses in civilian life. Despite the bombers' attempts to hide in the dark, German air defences became adept at directing spotlights, anti-aircraft fire, and German night fighters to the bomber streams. A large number of Allied bombers were shot down in any given raid. While a whole suite of technological and operational innovations attempted to improve targeting, navigation, and survivability in British Commonwealth bombers, it was not until the fall of 1944 that the deterioration of the German air defences resulted in a return to daylight raids.[2] So for much of the war, Canadians in Bomber Command were flying in the dark.

National identity was a natural rallying point, and men proudly wore their 'CANADA' shoulder flashes, distinguishing them from other British Commonwealth airmen. National distinctions were, however, somewhat muddled in bomber service. Men from the Dominion of Canada were serving in the RAF when the war broke out, and despite a push for the 'Canadianization' of Royal Canadian Air Force (RCAF) efforts overseas, many Canadians would fight in British RAF squadrons throughout the conflict. These early-war fliers would witness the many teething troubles in the development of Bomber Command's bite. Soon Canadian squadrons were added to the order of battle, but even these included Brits and others from across the British Commonwealth in their ranks. Eventually fifteen squadrons were formed under No. 6 (Canadian) Group, operating as a nominally all-Canadian formation. By 1944, Canadian personnel formed a quarter of those serving in Bomber Command.[3] By the end of the war they made up one third of the force. As the fictional Hank Dunfield confesses, the "romance of the air" encouraged many young Canadian men to sign up for the air force, inspired by dreams of flight and heroic stories of aces in the First World War or Battle of Britain. Likewise, some recruits avoided joining the infantry due to the well-known misery of the trenches during the First World War.[4] Many self-styled Billy Bishops hoped to become pilots, but the majority ended up serving as navigators, bomb aimers, wireless operators, air gunners, or flight engineers. RCAF airmen were all volunteers, and many signed up out of a sense of duty and righteousness. Others enlisted due to social pressures or even guaranteed pay, food, and lodging.

Canadian bomber squadrons, units comprised of hundreds of men, also adopted their own sub-identities, akin to those of the regiments of the army. Each developed heraldry, official mottos, and sometimes associations to particular Canadian localities that sponsored them. Formed on April 23, 1941, the first RCAF heavy bomber squadron in Bomber Command was No. 405 (Vancouver) Squadron. Its crest contained an eagle grasping quintessential Canadian flora: a cluster of maple leaves. The second operational squadron began a popular theme in selecting a North American animal for its identifier. No. 408 (Goose) Squadron displayed the proud Canadian Goose as its emblem. RCAF Station Linton-on-Ouse was dubbed 'The Goosepool.'[5] Eventually there were squadrons associated with the Snowy Owl, Bison, and Porcupine. Hank's 'Moose Squadron' might be catalogued here.

Due to wartime censorship, reportage surrounding squadron identities had to be veiled, but some reporters found a workaround in mentioning well-known commanding officers. There were perhaps none better known than Wing Commander John 'The Moose' Fulton of Kamloops, for whom No. 419 'Moose' Squadron acquired its nickname. Fulton was a pre-war RCAF officer who is said to have obtained the handle in 1934, when explaining to a senior RAF officer where he was from.[6] When he described the geography surrounding the interior BC city, the officer said, "I suppose that you have bagged your share of moose?" Not knowing what to say, Fulton replied in the affirmative, and the nickname stuck. Men in the squadron came to self-identify as 'Moosemen.' In 1944, citizens from the squadron's sponsor-city of Kamloops hunted and canned some 160 pounds of moose meat and sent it overseas. A feast was held on May 5, 1944, to celebrate becoming the first operational full-strength RCAF squadron to fly Canadian-built Lancasters exclusively.[7] The squadron identity long outlived Fulton, who was killed while accompanying his fliers in an operation over Hamburg on July 28, 1942. As historian John G. Armstrong wrote, Fulton's "fabled luck had finally succumbed to the grim statistical probabilities."[8]

Many commanding officers flew on bombing missions with their squadrons, as did the Air-Officer-Commanding, No. 6 Group, Air-Vice-Marshal C. M. 'Black Mike' McEwen. Doing so risked the lives of celebrated and skilled military commanders, but also proved to Canadian bomber crews that leaders were members of their perilous guild. In Braem's play, Hank loses his crew when he is grounded due to nervous anxiety. It was possible, also, to lose one's crew when leaders flew to prove their courage in solidarity with airmen; one pilot recalled that he and his tail gunner sat out a raid so a wing commander and gunnery officer could take their places, and the plane, and the rest of their crew, never returned.[9]

National and squadron identities were one way to draw men together and develop an *esprit de corps*, yet bonds between crew members were paramount. Aircrew shared terrifying risks on missions and relied on each other's competence to stay alive. While national or squadron identity were certainly sources of pride, it was the immediate group of an individual bomber's six or seven aircrew that formed the key social unit. Crews of weapons systems such as tanks had similar bonds, but the experience of flying in the dark, often in freezing conditions through heavy cloud, strengthened the ties between young men who together braced against enemy and elements.

The members of a crew were completely interdependent on each other's competencies. Survival was contingent on skilled pilots who needed to wrestle the heavy bombers full of thousands of pounds of explosives and aviation fuel through take-offs and landings in treacherous flying conditions, not to mention the evasion of flak and fighters. Yet survival also required every other member of the crew to perform their duties: plotting a course through danger and back again; peering into darkness for approaching night fighters; and operating an increasingly complex array of new technology for navigation, communications, and radar purposes.

When pilot J. Douglas Harvey of 408 (Goose) Squadron received his promotion, he lobbied for the rest of his crew to be commissioned as officers as well, stating, "Why not? They do the same job as I do."[10] Each crewman's job was to perform his vital role within the roaring machine that defied gravity, dropped death from above, and attempted to return intact. Performing their function efficiently was paramount; to let down their crew could mean annihilation for all.

Bomber crews underwent an interesting social experiment in their formation that might be considered one of the earliest interventions of *fortuna*, or chance, in their war experience. The process of 'crewing up' involved herding large groups of airmen with the right ratio of trades into a hangar and letting them sort themselves out into crews. A social whim would begin bonds that sometimes lasted a lifetime. Men milled about and sized each other up, trying to assess competence and compatibility at a glance. Navigator Robert Kensett, who flew in Halifax bombers with No. 158 Squadron RAF, remembered the icebreaker, "How would you like a shit-hot pilot?"[11]

Aircrew selected the men they would fight the war with and, in some cases, die with. Nicknames were terms of endearment and were often chalked on the sides of aircraft close to each crewman's position. As historian Tim Cook writes, "as part of laddish culture, nearly everyone had a nickname . . . New recruits were being remade into warriors, but first they had to be renamed by one another."[12]

Wireless air gunner Glen Hancock of Wolfville, Nova Scotia, recalled the crewing up process,

> No unwelcome bodies were forced upon us. We considered personality, age, attitude, and even marital status. Some airmen had a thing about a married man being a better crew member because he would want to return to his family and wouldn't do anything foolish that would jeopardize the safety of the crew. This was nonsense. We were assembled in a compound, like a herd of cattle being selected for their breeding qualities.[13]

Of his crew, which hailed from Toronto, Peterborough, Dauphin (Manitoba), Calgary, Wolfville, and London (England), Hancock's memories recall youthful arrogance and a poetic sense of their fate:

> This was the 'Gen Crew,' by our own estimation the most competent crew in Bomber Command. Fate had thrown us together, to 'slip the surly bonds of earth,' and top 'the wind-swept heights with easy grace / where never lark, or even eagle flew . . . ' We would do the rest of the war together, with our lives, our very souls bonded together.[14]

Once they progressed through myriad training units, and finally got off the ground together on their first operations, crews would hear the steady roar of the engines and some banter over the intercom set before they came over enemy territory. Oxygen masks were needed above ten thousand feet. Then it was silence and waiting for what may come, punctuated by the navigator's directions on the approach to target. The rear gunner, 'Tail-End Charlie' in aircrew parlance, scanned the night skies for threats from what one veteran called "the coldest, loneliest place in the world."[15] Since fighters often approached from the rear, intercom silence might be pierced by the rear gunner's call for evasive maneuvers, accompanied by the sound of his guns firing. Despite his electric-heated suit, his position was cold and isolated. Bailing out of a damaged burning aircraft was a risky maneuver for all crew, but rear gunners had extra clothing bundled about them as they tried to put on the parachute stored outside their turret. Policy advised them to traverse the whole aircraft and jump from the front door hatch. If they needed to bail out quicker, or fire or other obstacles blocked the long walk, they could try the rear crew entry door on the Lancaster or spin their turret so they could exit out of the tail itself. Their chances of survival could be diminished by equipment malfunction, explosive fuel and ordnance, and centrifugal forces pinning them to the fuselage.

Many men vividly recall the pyrotechnic spectacle of coloured target indication flares, tracer rounds, searchlights, and planes exploding in the night. The fictional Hank Dunfield's memories align well with the men who survived to tell the tale of fire and brimstone in the skies above Germany. Jerrold Morris recalled,

> the most alarming factor of the German defences was undoubtedly the searchlights. They had master beams, radar controlled during the preliminary search . . . Once caught, every searchlight in range would fix you, and wiggle and squirm as you might, you couldn't shake them off. Then the guns joined in and filled the apex of the cone with bursts; it was a terrifying thing to watch. All too often, the sequel was a small flame, burning bright as the aircraft fell towards the ground . . . Everyone dreaded being coned.[16]

Anti-aircraft fire ('flak') bursts would often become intense closer to the target. Berlin was defended by some two thousand anti-aircraft guns.[17] As pilot Bob Pratt bluntly stated, "It scared the hell out of you, to be exact. And anyone who wasn't scared of it is not here with us today."[18] Historians Spencer Dunmore and William Carter describe the approach to bombing targets: "Flak was like a succession of electric lights snapping on and off in mid-air, the nearest ones emitting a dull 'woof' that was just audible over the roar of the engines. A sharp stink of explosive. An occasional patter as spent fragments of flak hit the fuselage."[19] If the bomber made it to the target area, the bomb aimer would guide the pilot to the target in an excruciating two-minutes when the plane needed to be kept level, and then report "bombs gone." Then for another thirty-second eternity the plane had to remain on a steady course for the cameras that took photographs of the target upon explosion.

In Braem's *Flight Risk*, Hank draws on his war experience to help Sarah acknowledge her own fears. During the Second World War, Canadian pilot Malcolm MacConnell arrived at a similar acceptance of his dread during his service in the RAF. He recalled, "I had a very good crew, but with the flak and fighters around, I felt fear — deep fear, terror. But after a little experience, I found that I was able to cope — recognize the fear, recognize everything happening in my surroundings and sort of cope and react and do things."[20] One crew member recalled his rear gunner worrying about his fears impeding his ability in the air: he "was always frightened, but his greatest concern was that his fear would impair his ability as an air gunner. He suffered phobia gallantly."[21]

Hank Dunfield is proud of his twenty-four missions completed during the war. A mission count was important for several reasons: it was a clear indicator of experience, and it served as a countdown to relief from flying potentially deadly operations. Bomber Command acknowledged that men could only endure a certain amount of time as operational aircrew; it was accepted that they deserved a break from constant threat and the punishing routine of flying. In the early years of the war, an airman was considered done his flying duties at two hundred operational hours (around twenty-five sorties of eight hours each), whereby he was taken off operational flying.[22] In August 1942, the bar for a complete tour was set at thirty sorties. After that a man was given less arduous service and possibly even sent back to Canada.

In May 1943, however, service was divided into a first tour of thirty missions, and then a second tour of twenty. In between, there was a break for desk duties or training of at least six months. There was good reason to keep track and hope that one made it to thirty missions. Some who made it to the benchmark, however, lamented that their crews would be broken up and likely never fly together again.[23] Wartime psychologists identified major stress points surrounding three phases of the tour: the opening few sorties when the perils were new; the mid-way point around twelve to fourteen missions when it seemed that luck must be running out; and the last few missions of a tour, when some hope returned that they might actually live through the experience.[24] That seemed too good to be true. In May 1944, a points system was developed, whereby less dangerous missions were awarded a lower score. As John Fitzgerald, a Canadian air gunner on a RAF Lancaster wrote home, "these targets in France . . . each trip consists of only one third of a op. [operation] which is silly because if you go over there and get killed you don't get only one third killed."[25]

Death was a constant feature of the bombing campaigns, and it was all too obvious to the fliers. One airman recalled sleeping in the bed of a man who had perished the night before.[26] Newly arriving crew were told there were no beds, but not to worry, the air crews were on 'ops' that night and there would be bunks available for them in the morning.[27] No. 428 (Ghost) Squadron stands out for its fatalistic heraldry, featuring a skeletal ghost. Most sources suggest the name was selected due to its deployment on night missions, but when navigator Ernie Dickson arrived as a 'sprog' (untried novice), he was told that the ghostly name was selected because all their aircrew ended up dead.[28]

While squadron initiations could take such grim turns, the statistics also told a gruesome tale. In June 1943, when the Canadians of No. 6 Group were flying Wellington bombers, they suffered an average of 9 per cent losses each mission.[29] In January 1944, losses averaged 7.3 per cent per sortie.[30] At that rate, only 10 per cent of crews would survive a thirty-operation tour. At the loss rates of 1943, only 2.5 per cent of Bomber Command aircrew would see the end of their second tour. Losses of over 5 per cent were considered unsustainable: force morale would collapse. As the war progressed, the chances of survival improved. No. 6

Group averaged a loss rate of 2 per cent over the whole bomber campaign.[31] Of the forty thousand Canadians who served in Bomber Command, 8,240 were killed on operations, amounting to 20.6 per cent.

Death could come in the form of one's crewmate horribly maimed and mutilated inside the aircraft, but for brother crews, death also snuck in during darkness. As Flight Lieutenant John Zinkhan recalled, "You never saw your friends actually die. They were just missing from the station the next day."[32]

Historian Tim Cook writes, "After a sortie, lockers were emptied. Names came off the roster board. And the war went on. Of course chums missed chums, but the distressing losses required a callousness for dealing with those who never returned from the night-time operations."[33] Navigator Robert Kensett's memoirs record denial and repression of the pain and fear of losing friends in the squadron:

> When you were flying ops, death was a distinct possibility, but aircrew would not even consider this fact. They would not admit it even if someone on the squadron were killed. They simply made believe that he was not in his usual place. He wasn't in his billet, the mess or anywhere around; he was simply away somewhere.[34]

Tail gunner Gordon Hunt recalled losing many friends on 'shaky dos' (raids with lots of flak or fighters),

> I lost a lot of my buddies on those two raids [on Dusseldorf] and many more on the two raids on Revigny, another hot target. It was not pleasant to see all the empty bunks and service people gathering all the crew's effects — not pleasant at all. But because of the times and our youth, we never thought that we might be next. I will say, however, that I would do it

all over again, serving with the finest bunch of men anywhere in the world.[35]

While men were badly injured and returned to base in damaged aircraft, the low ratio of casualties to those killed in bomber service suggests it was an all or nothing game. Pilot Geoff Marlow recalled the many ways to 'get the chop' on operations,

> some had gone without warning when their bomb load exploded from impact with the ground or another plane. Others went down with their bombers burning from end to end, spinning wildly out of control, unable to bail out because of injury or being trapped within the aircraft. Others had feverishly managed to abandon ship, only to float down into the freezing cold of the wintry sea or into a mob of infuriated civilians seeking revenge for the loss of their homes or loved ones.[36]

Confidence in the equipment that service personnel operate has long buoyed morale and enabled them to carry on in dangerous situations. The Lancaster was the preferred bomber in British Commonwealth service and a point of pride for their crews. In his last letter home to his family in New Westminster, BC, John Fitzgerald wrote, "What is the idea of saying I was in a Halifax bomber. Now that is an insult to us "Lancaster!" boys and there is a sore point between the Hally & Lanc squadrons. So don't make the mistake again cause we are in aeroplanes and not flying Jalopies (Hallies)."[37] The Lancaster was flying active missions by the end of 1941. From August 1941 to October 1942 Halifax crews were lost at twice the rate as those in Lancasters.[38] Later models of the Halifaxes, however, improved their failings so that there was little advantage to either craft.[39]

Crews seemed to champion whichever machine they happened to fly, and planes took on identities of their own, embellished by nose art or paintings on their fuselage. Official call signs were based on the phonetic alphabet used by the Royal Air Force, so while air traffic controllers and operations room plotters might use 'C for Charlie' or 'F for Freddie,' for aircraft, they still might be given other nicknames and were universally coded feminine by the crews. Often the radio alphabet guided the nickname. 'Q for Queen' meant that there were often variations on the royal theme: 'Queen of them All,' 'Queen O' the Swamp,' or simply 'Queenie.' 'Pranging Queenie,' a Halifax III of No. 433 Squadron, managed to survive the war without a fatal 'prang' (crash). Other plane names seem motivated by youthful lust. 'E for Easy' revealed that many men dreamt of carefree nights. In *Flight Risk*, 'Mollie's Legs' encapsulates one major theme of nose art, as "pin-up girls and other risqué subjects" were the most prominent forms of personalization.[40]

Some nose art and aircraft names laughed in the face of death and killing. At times it was hard to know whether images of death were aggressive threats towards the enemy or a fatalism about their own lives. Grim reapers, skeletons, vultures, and devils abounded on nose art. Bomber crews risked their own lives delivering death. Just about everything in a flier's world was encoded in an insider's slang and some of it took a sardonic tone towards the tools of the trade. A common bomb used in Canadian service — a four-thousand-pound cocktail of high-explosive TNT and ammonium nitrate — was granted the euphemism 'cookie.'[41] The industrialized Ruhr Valley and its formidable anti-aircraft defences was 'Happy Valley.' Cartoons were a common theme for nose art, and 'Bambi,' seems a particularly ironic name for a machine whose purpose was to incinerate a city. Other slang was dark. Ambulances which might race to aircraft with injured airmen were 'blood wagons' or 'meat wagons.'

Historian David Bashow has described casualties in the bombing campaign as "unrelenting, bloody, and depressingly random."[42] With the chances of death on any given sortie in the dark winter of 1943-44, at somewhere around one in twenty, it is no surprise that crews reached for good luck charms to ward off death. As Hank suggests, urinating on one of the bomber's wheels was a natural relief before a long flight and became one of innumerable rituals. A

Canadian navigator flying in an RAF squadron recalled their pilot licking his hand and slapping one of the bombs before every take-off.[43] The routine of checking equipment ensured that the complex machines were ready for flight, but also helped calm the complex of emotions for men who would soon face clawing searchlights, flak, and night fighters. Good luck talismans came in many forms: stockings or scarves gifted by lovers, dolls, pipe-cleaner leprechauns, and rabbit's feet. Religious icons like rosaries or Saint Christopher medals straddled the line between good luck charms and objects of faith. Airmen called on God or good luck to see them through.

Clint Seeley, a mid-upper gunner from Kingston recalled his prayers moderated for air service: "Though I am flying through the skies in the shadow of death, I fear no evil, for thou art with me, thy rod and staff they comfort me."[44]

Glen Hancock recalls that the padre would ride his bike along to the dispersal sights and offer a short prayer. He notes, "We would say our own prayers as well, but they were never ostentatious."[45] Some crews would be sure to board the aircraft in a specific order.[46]

Tim Cook writes, "All such magical thinking helped to ward off fear of the unknown. With so little control over their destiny, airmen hoped that items imbued with a sort of other-world power— which they had discovered or cultivated—would protect them." [47]

Painful loss was also internalized as bad luck. Pilot Bob Turnbull, of Govan, Saskatchewan, wrote his future wife, sadly reporting the loss of a good friend. "Cause unknown/Talking to him not twenty minutes before it happened and saw them take-off and then crash. What a strange world of fortune this can be — things happen so suddenly and leave you with such lost feelings that are impossible to describe. And still we fly on."[48] He tied a lock of his sweetheart's hair inside his flying scarf for good luck. Some nose art featured images of dice in recognition of the role of luck. 'Lucky Lady,' a Lancaster from No. 425 Squadron combined two popular themes.

Air service in Bomber Command seemed to age men quickly, wearing their nerves down to thinly frayed sinews. Some began to get the shakes, have nightmares, or experience other symptoms of long-standing anxiety.[49] A medical officer might apply barbiturates to affect a deep sleep for as much as a day. Only one in a hundred men would get so bad that they could no longer fly, and fewer than that were labelled with the stigmatizing diagnosis 'lack of moral fibre (LMF).' This term was coined in September 1941 as a pejorative for those who were not able to carry on and refused to fly. It was considered akin to 'malingering.' Some officers were kind and took a man off air service if they saw he could no longer take it, but there were cruel incidences where men were shamed on the parade square, their flying badges ripped from their uniforms. Our fictional flier Hank Dunfield admits that he was under suspicion of LMF during the war, which suggests that despite his fond memories of the excitement and camaraderie of wartime service, there were profoundly negative experiences to his war as well.

Some tail gunners broke down after stressful service. Robert Kensett wrote, "Our rear gunner, the placid Yorkshire farm boy, had heart palpitations and a nervous breakdown, and he was shipped off to hospital. We did not see him again. Apparently, the strain of peering out into unfriendly skies, especially at night, for five days and nights straight, had been too much for him."[50]

Recent assessments have suggested that the deaths of Canadian airmen were not in vain: that despite being a crude instrument, strategic bombing diverted German resources from other fighting fronts and deteriorated war industry.[51] The bombers of No. 6 Group flew 40,822 'ops' and dropped 126,122 tons of bombs during the war.[52] Half of Germany's urban areas were completely destroyed. Millions of people were rendered homeless and over three hundred thousand were killed. The cost was great for No. 6 Group as well; 814 bombers were lost in this apocalyptic clash. Across Bomber Command, 9,919 Canadians lost their lives.

Then it was over. After 1945, it was back to 'civvy street' for the survivors of Bomber Command. As Glen Hancock interpreted it,

> The peace challenged the world to make those sacrifices
> meaningful . . . Thousands of veteran airmen, who had
> lived so long on the edge, suddenly found themselves

responsible for making decisions on their own and for preparing themselves to manage their leftover lives. Many of them were not up to it. They had stood up to the confrontation of death, but they could not meet the challenges of life. They had felt important when they were [bombing] cities and tasting cordite. Now they were back to where they started, prepared for nothing.[53]

Hancock recognizes that most made the transition well, with many becoming Canadian leaders during a generation of opportunity. Yet: "Those who failed to make the transition became a different kind of war casualty. Their marriages failed, their dreams evaporated. But they shared with their comrades the conviction that they had fought a just war for a grateful country. And there would never be anything in their lives that would eclipse that greatest adventure of all."[54] Such testimony is particularly applicable to *Flight Risk*'s Hank, who wrestles with demons and drink after his war service.

Like Hank, historical airmen have spoken of their own lifelong mourning. Don Cheney, of Ottawa, who flew in the RAF's 617 Squadron, wanted to make this clear: "As a final note, something that is fundamental to my experience is that three of my crew were killed in action, and that's with me every day. They're with me every day. They're still alive, and they're still twenty-two years old."[55]

Doug Bashow writes that,

Many veterans carry the scars, both physical and mental, of their wartime experiences. None who lived through these events has remained untouched by them. While a number have such painful memories of the war that they refuse to talk about it, far more have said that, in spite of the grave dangers and the dreadful casualties incurred, they have never felt more alive than they did during that period of their lives.[56]

Bashow notes that a few were stricken by survivor's guilt, but more treat their survival as a gift and live life to its fullest.

Some, like Hank Dunfield, kept their uniforms. Time could take its toll. A veteran wrote, "Some years later I opened my trunk that I had kept in the cellar and took out my cap that I had worn so proudly. There was some mould on the brim, and the insignia fell off onto the floor. Obviously my air force career was over."[57] Yet, in a way, it was never really over. It seems that some men, like Braem's character, were stuck in the war. The contrast between the safety and boredom of old age and visceral memories of the war years is one reason for returning to the past. Indelible memories of the men who helped each other carry on is another. In the case of Hank, philosophies of wartime survival are unearthed as he counsels his new friend and nurse. Perhaps he regrets a period of his life when he was doing his best to drown out his war ghosts. He longs for the comradery of those days yet can find no greater moral purpose that justifies how things ended up. Not everything happens for a reason. Glen Hancock's memoir of his war years with No. 408 'Goose' Squadron ends with sensory memories of his youth and a touching tribute to his crew:

> I can hear the sound of engines warming up at daybreak. I can hear the sound of glasses clinking in a thousand British pubs and the enchanting laughter of pretty girls . . . I can taste those operational bacon-and-egg meals. I can see the boyish faces of my crew, my dearest friends. They are all gone now . . . Now they belong to the ages. I can hear the symbolic 'Last Post,' acknowledging all the magnificent young men on my squadron who missed the chance to grow up.[58]

Halifax bomber "I'm Easy" of No. 426 "Thunderbird" Squadron Royal Canadian Air Force, ca. 1944–45. Photo courtesy Bomber Command Museum, Nanton, Alberta.

Aircrew from 424 Squadron RCAF, with their Halifax bomber "Dipsy Doodle." Left to right: Mid-upper gunner Flight Sergeant Peter Engbrecht, rear gunner Flight Sergeant Gordon Gillanders, and pilot, Flight Sergeant James G. Keys. Engbrecht was a Mennonite who did not adhere to pacifism, shooting down at least six enemy aircraft during the war. In total, Gillanders and Engbrecht accounted for nine confirmed enemy aircraft destroyed and another two probables. Photo courtesy Bomber Command Museum, Nanton, Alberta.

Unidentified rear gunner of a Lancaster bomber. Photo courtesy Bomber Command Museum, Nanton, Alberta.

The crew of a Halifax bomber of No. 420 Squadron Royal Canadian Air Force. The aircraft completed forty-six operations and crashed near Tholthorpe, England on 19 July 1944, killing the Canadian pilot Stanley J. Joplin, Australian wireless operator G. H. Minchin, British flight engineer N. J. Shand, air gunner Wilfred Stanley Barnard, and rear gunner Gerald A. Kent. Photo courtesy Bomber Command Museum, Nanton, Alberta.

The crew of a Halifax bomber of No. 408 "Goose" Squadron Royal Canadian Air Force poses in front of their aircraft "Vicky the Vicious Virgin," ca. 1944. The pilot, third from left, is Ron Craven, the flight engineer, second from the right, is Chinese Canadian Charles Wong. Bomb aimer Herb Evans is also likely in the photograph. Evans was the artist who drew the nose art on aircraft. Photo courtesy Bomber Command Museum, Nanton, Alberta.

Per Ardua Ad Astra

David B. Hogan MD, FRCPC and Philip D. St. John MD, FRCPC

In January of 1940, at the start of the Second World War, Stephen Leacock wrote a grim piece about turning seventy, in which he describes old age as akin to crossing no man's land between two opposing trenches:

> As we have moved forward the tumult that now lies behind us has died down. The sounds grow less and less. It is almost silence. There is an increasing feeling of isolation, of being alone. We seem so far apart. Here and there one falls, silently, and lies a little bundle on the ground that the rolling mist is burying. Can we not keep nearer? It's hard to see one another. Can you hear me? Call to me. I am alone. This must be near the end.[1]

When Leacock wrote these words, there was relatively little societal interest in the study of aging and the care of older persons. One reason was that old age was not a very common phenomenon. Only around 7 per cent of the Canadian population at that time was sixty-five years or older, compared to the some 29 per cent that was less than fifteen.[2] Edmund Cowdry (1888-1975), born in Fort MacLeod, Alberta, was an exception in calling for more attention. In 1937, he convinced the Josiah Macy Jr. Foundation, in the United States, to fund a conference on aging research. The published proceedings of this gathering, *Problems of Ageing* (1939), heralded the emergence of gerontology (the study of the social, cultural, psychological, cognitive, and biological aspects of aging) as a legitimate field of inquiry. In 1944, Cowdry presciently called for all medical trainees to be instructed in geriatrics (the branch of medicine dealing with the health and care of older people) and for the creation of a cadre of specialists to do the teaching.[3] The same year, the Gerontologic Unit at the Allan Memorial Institute in Montreal was established for the study of the psychiatric problems associated with aging.[4] These initial forays, though, did not have wide impact.

We live now in a very different world, where more and more of us are coming to grips with the challenges of our later years. The proportion of older persons in the general population has now increased nearly three-fold to around 19 per cent, while that of children has dropped to about one in six.[5] The shift has seen increased interest in gerontology and geriatrics, and basic and applied research on aging have both expanded rapidly. The former includes longitudinal studies, in which individuals are followed over time, providing information that can lead to a better understanding of the determinants of aging well and the antecedents of the chronic diseases frequently encountered in our later years. One such study has followed Canadian aircrews from the Second World War — men like *Flight Risk*'s reluctant centenarian, Hank Dunfield.

During most of the Second World War (1939-1945), Group Captain Francis Alexander Lavens (Frank) Mathewson (1905-1994) was the deputy director of medical services for the Royal Canadian Air Force (RCAF).[6] A physician interested in cardiology, he carried out fitness evaluations of approximately seven thousand RCAF male recruits who enlisted during this time. This assessment included a medical history (that surprisingly, to us, didn't include asking about their smoking status), physical examination (including height, weight, and blood pressure), and, what was unique for the time, a resting electrocardiogram.[7] Because of the high quality of information collected, researchers discussed setting up a long-term study that would utilize it.[8] The study would focus in particular on the future significance of electrocardiographic abnormalities found in otherwise healthy individuals.

Between 1946 and 1948, surviving RCAF aircrew members plus a small group of non-military pilots were contacted and invited to participate in a longitudinal study focusing on cardiovascular disease. A total of 3,983 men with an average age of thirty-one (90 per cent ranged in age from twenty to thirty-nine) were eventually enrolled as of July 1, 1948. The Manitoba Follow-up Study (MFUS) participants were from around the country and in some instances outside it (the study is named for the University of Manitoba, where its records were and are housed). The study has continued for over seventy-two years since then. By July 1, 2018, of the nearly four thousand originally enrolled, 3,846 had passed away. The remaining 137 were still being followed.[9]

The MFUS's participants have shown remarkable dedication, calling themselves 'Mathewson's guinea pigs.'[10] In a book about the MFUS, the participants refer to themselves as study members, rather than subjects.[11] In 1983, federal funding for the study was terminated because MFUS was deemed to have run its course. The study members and staff disagreed. The former collectively chipped in about sixty thousand dollars annually and remained the study's primary source of funding from 1983 until 1996.[12] Some members continue to donate to the registered charity they established to support it. Another reflection of their dedication to the study has been the retention rate. In 1998, fifty years after the study commenced, fewer than 3 per cent of those initially enrolled had been lost to follow-up.[13]

Initially participants were contacted every five years, but as they aged, the frequency increased to first every three years, then yearly, twice a year, and finally three times a year. The data collected have varied over the course of the study and include survival status, results of medical examinations, and surveys obtaining information on occupation, retirement, income, physical activity, and other lifestyle factors (such as smoking), and open-ended questions about wartime experiences and their long-term effects. In 1996, the average age of the around two thousand surviving participants was seventy-six. In response to their movement into the latter part of life, the research focus of the study shifted to exploring the multidimensional concept of successful aging. The researchers added their Successful Aging Questionnaire (SAQ), which captured information on living arrangements, activities of daily living, quality of life, and definitions of successful aging as defined by the participants. They introduced a nutritional risk survey in 2007, and five items about frailty (which denotes a state of heightened vulnerability) in 2015.[14]

Research results at first dealt with cardiovascular disease.[15] More recent MFUS publications have reflected the shift to successful aging[16] and other aspects of older age.[17] When initially asked in 1996, most (83.8 per cent) MFUS participants who responded felt they had aged successfully.[18] Common components of their personal definitions of successful aging were good health, a happy and satisfying life, keeping active (physically, mentally, and/or socially), a positive outlook, having a close and loving circle of family and friends, and independence. These components have remained consistent at a group and individual level over time.[19]

Could the fictional Hank Dunfield have been a MFUS member? The answer would have to be an unqualified yes. He was an RCAF aircrew member during the Second World War and of the right age. If he turned one hundred in 2017, when the play had its première, he would have been thirty-one in 1948 (the average age at entry for 'Mathewson's guinea pigs'). We don't know where the play is set, but taking a hint from the name of his residence (Ponderosa Pine Lodge Seniors Care Centre), it is probably in Alberta or British Columbia. As mentioned previously, MFUS participants came from across Canada and were not limited to those living in Manitoba.

Though the MFUS did not directly address mental health issues, Hank's story suggests that he has post-traumatic stress disorder (what he calls "LMF, Lack of Moral Fibre") with survivor's guilt, which occurs when a person believes they have done something wrong by surviving a traumatic event when others did not. While he was grounded after his twenty-fourth mission, Hank's plane was shot down with a replacement tail gunner; hence, his leaving the lodge at night was to go and wait for his "plane to come in." Symptoms of survivor's guilt include depression, mood swings, social withdrawal, sleep disturbances and nightmares — characteristics he shows. This sense of guilt is chronic and can increase in intensity with aging.

The MFUS found much person-to-person variability in perceptions of frailty.[20] Hank's impaired mobility, disability, depressed mood, impaired cognition, and suspected dementia (prior to his lodge admission he was financially exploited while memory issues and sundowning are referred to frequently in the play) and multiple morbidities (prostate, back, hip [fracture], lungs, heart) would likely mark him in our eyes (and possibly his) as frail. These features in addition to the tedium, isolation, loss of independence, control ("No one asked me if this is what I wanted"), and anything pleasurable in his life speak against him experiencing at the start of the play successful aging as defined by MFUS members. Hank makes it clear he resents being over-protected and doesn't want a lingering death ("I wish you'd just let me go", ". . . [I've been here] too long").

Near the end of Scene 11, at a pivotal point in the play, Hank quotes the RCAF motto, "*Per Ardua Ad Astra*" (through adversity to the stars). He reflects on it, and concludes "we did see some stars." How we deal with the often unequal and at times unfair adversity we encounter in our lives influences our ability to live and age successfully. Some emerge relatively unscathed through these trials[21] while others must make choices and accept adaptions in order to maximize their sense of well-being while minimizing the effects of declining health.[22]

Completing the model of the Lancaster bomber is a running theme in the play and a link in the relationship between Hank and Sarah. The model is completed when the two place a 'Mollie's Legs' decal on the plane. On the wall of Mathewson's office at the University of Manitoba,[23] he displays the image of a Lancaster bomber, presented to him by MFUS members. The decal below the cockpit depicts the wave pattern of an electrocardiogram.[24]

Director's Notes

Samantha MacDonald

In the spring of 2016, before we began our Stage One workshop, Meg and I sat down to talk about the *Flight Risk* — about whose story it was, what the journeys were, why these people needed each other in this moment, what they could learn from each other. On that sunny afternoon, Meg said something that I will never forget. She told me, "These characters are stars in constellation." It was a perfect reflection.

In the course of this play each character shines on the others, feels the gravitational pull of the others, and orbits the others, for better or for worse, without much to say about it. And I think that's pretty true for all of us.

I lost my mother when I was twenty-two years old; she is a star whose gravitational pull has never dwindled in my life. I have friends who are thousands of miles away, and still we shine on each other. Hank has lost so much, and the pull of those stars is inexorable. Sarah and Kathleen contend with their own darkly shining stars.

The play reminds us that if we can move through the adversity of our own lives, the stars are there. As angry, as hurt, as broken as we can sometimes be, we each have the opportunity to shine, and to make a difference for someone else. So often in life we find just the right person at just the right time, as Hank and Sarah do. And somehow, with the glow of that other star lighting our path, we find our way.

And at the end of the day, the beautiful message Meg leaves us with is this: we are all out there in that great big sky shining *together* . . . stars in constellation.

I am so very grateful to have played a part in the growth of this extraordinary piece, which will soon have a life far beyond our little cluster of stars — so grateful and so proud. Thank you to everyone in our small but mighty constellation for making this process so sweet. *Per Ardua Ad Astra*, indeed.

Original Cast, Direction, and Crew

Flight Risk was developed at Lunchbox Theatre as part of the 2016 Suncor Stage One Festival of New Works. The play premiered at the Lunchbox Theatre in Calgary on October 23, 2017.

Cast
Hank Dunfield: Christopher Hunt
Sarah Baker: Kristen Padayas
Kathleen Shore: Kathryn Kerbes

Direction
Director: Samantha MacDonald
RBC Emerging Director: Chris Stockton

Crew
Scenic and Costume Design: Derek Paulich
Sound Design: Aiden Lytton
Lighting Design: Lisa Floyd
Lighting Assistant: Tristan Lavacque
Stage Manager: Kennedy Greene

Notes

FOREWORD

1 Sick + Twisted, "About," https://www.sickandtwisted.ca/about, accessed October 7, 2022.

2 Arthur W. Frank, *The Wounded Storyteller* (Chicago, University of Chicago Press: 1995), 134.

FLYING IN THE DARK: THE CANADIAN BOMBER COMMAND EXPERIENCE AND MEG BRAEM'S *FLIGHT RISK*

1 "Mass Murder in Guernica," *New York Times*, April 29, 1937, 20; "Basque Horror Laid to Nazi Fliers," *The Globe and Mail*, April 28, 1937.

2 Laurie Peloquin, "Area Bombing by Day: Bomber Command and the Daylight Offensive, 1944–1945," *Canadian Military History* 15, no. 3 (2006), 31.

3 Tim Cook, *The Necessary War: Canadians Fighting the Second World War* (Toronto: Penguin, 2014), 162.

4 Cook, *The Necessary War*, 159-60.

5 John G. Armstrong, "RCAF Identity in Bomber Command: Squadron Names and Sponsors," *Canadian Military History* 8, no. 2 (1999): 47.

6 Stéphane Guevremont, *Moosa Aswayita 'Beware of the Moose': A History of 419 Squadron 'City of Kamloops' 1941-2016* (Cold Lake: 419 Squadron RCAF, 2016), 17.

7 Guevremont, *Moosa Aswayita*, 204.

8 John G. Armstrong, "RCAF Identity in Bomber Command: Squadron Names and Sponsors," *Canadian Military History* 8, no. 2 (1999): 45.

9 Arthur B. Wahlroth of Toronto, flying Wellingtons with No. 405 Squadron, quoted in *Flying Under Fire Volume Two: More Aviation Tales from the Second World War*, ed. William J. Wheeler (Calgary: Fifth House, 2003), 45-46.

10 Quoted in Spencer Dunmore and William Carter, *Reap the Whirlwind: The Untold Story of 6 Group, Canada's Bomber Force of World War II* (Toronto: McClelland and Stewart, 1991), 59.

11 Robert C. Kensett, *A Walk in the Valley* (Burnstown: General Store Publishing, 2003), 34.

12 Cook, *The Necessary War*, 163.

13 Glen Hancock, *Charley Goes to War* (Kentville: Gaspereau Press, 2004), 189.

14 Hancock, *Charley Goes to War*, 190.

15 Fraser Muir of Westville, Nova Scotia, veteran of No. 50 Squadron RAF, as quoted in *We Were Freedom: Canadian Stories of the Second World War* (Toronto: Key Porter, 2010), 30.

16 As quoted in David L. Bashow, *No Prouder Place: Canadians and the Bomber Command Experience 1939-1945* (St. Catharines: Vanwell, 2005), 76.

17 Tim Cook, *Fight to the Finish: Canadians in the Second World War 1944-45* (Toronto: Penguin, 2015), 159-60.

18 As quoted in David L. Bashow, *No Prouder Place,* 192.

19 Dunmore and Carter, *Reap the Whirlwind,* 27.

20 As quoted in *We Were Freedom: Canadian Stories of the Second World War* (Toronto: Key Porter, 2010), 170.

21 Hancock, *Charley Goes to War,* 221.

22 Cook, *Fight to the Finish,* 26.

23 Dunmore and Carter, *Reap the Whirlwind,* 264.

24 Bashow, *No Prouder Place,* 215.

25 John Fitzgerald to mother and sister, May 18th, 1944, Canada Letters and Images Project, https://www.canadianletters.ca/content/document-11282; Dunmore and Carter, *Reap the Whirlwind,* 266.

26 Cook, *The Necessary War,* 199.

27 The story about the soon-to-be-available beds has been attributed to both 428 'Ghost' Squadron and 429 'Bison' Squadron. David L. Bashow, *No Prouder Place,* 214; Dunmore and Carter, *Reap the Whirlwind,* 62.

28 Dunmore and Carter, *Reap the Whirlwind,* 62.

29 Cook, *The Necessary War,* 314, 316.

30 Cook, *Fight to the Finish,* 19.

31 Bashow, *No Prouder Place,* 457-58.

32 As quoted in Cook, *Fight to the Finish,* 22.

33 Cook, *Fight to the Finish,* 22.

34   Robert C. Kensett, *A Walk in the Valley*, 99.

35   As quoted in *We Went Where They Sent Us . . . and did as we were told (most of the time)* ed. Gordon Bell (Lantzville: Oolichan Books, 2000), 245.

36   As quoted in Bashow, *No Prouder Place*, 13.

37   John Fitzgerald to mother and sister, August 17th, 1944, Canada Letters and Images Project, https://www.canadianletters.ca/content/document-11251.

38   Cook, *The Necessary War*, 202.

39   The introduction of the Hercules engine to the Halifax III in late 1943 is said to have been a turning point in their reputation. Dunmore and Carter, *Reap the Whirlwind*, 101.

40   Caitlin McWilliams, "Camaraderie, Morale and Material Culture: Reflections on the Nose Art of No. 6 Group Royal Canadian Air Force," *Canadian Military History* 19, no. 4 (Autumn 2010), 22.

41   Bashow, *No Prouder Place*, 527

42   Bashow, *No Prouder Place*, 180.

43   Kensett, *A Walk in the Valley*, 58.

44   As quoted Bashow, *No Prouder Place*, 180.

45   Hancock, *Charley Goes to War*, 221.

46   Bashow, *No Prouder Place*, 187.

47   Cook, *The Necessary War*, 231-32.

48   As quoted Bashow, *No Prouder Place*, 60.

49   Cook, *Fight to the Finish*, 28-29.

50   Kensett, *A Walk in the Valley*, 81.

51   Cook, *Fight to the Finish*, 7-8; 370-71.

52   Cook, *Fight to the Finish*, 374-375.

53   Hancock, *Charley Goes to War*, 297.

54   Hancock, *Charley Goes to War*, 298.

55   Quoted in Blake Heathcote, *Testaments of Honour: Personal Histories of Canada's War Veterans* (Toronto: Doubleday, 2002), 172.

56   Bashow, *No Prouder Place*, 452, 453.

57   Kensett, *A Walk in the Valley*, 118.

58   Hancock, *Charley Goes to War*, 298.

1   Stephen Leacock, "Three Score and Ten," *The Spectator*, January 19, 1940, 72-73.

2   John Ibbitson, "Older, Longer: The Super-Aging of Canadians Has Taken Everyone by Surprise," *The Globe and Mail* January 26, 2020. Accessed September 26, 2020, https://www.theglobeandmail.com/opinion/article-older-longer-the-super-aging-of-canadians-has-taken-everyone-by/.

3   David B. Hogan, "History of Geriatrics in Canada," *Canadian Bulletin of Medical History* 24, no. 1 (2007): 131-150.

4   K. Stern, "Observations in an Old Age Counselling Center. Preliminary Report on The First 100 Clients: Preliminary Report on The First 100 Clients," *Journal of Gerontology*, 3, no. 1 (1948): 48–60, https://doi.org/10.1093/geronj/3.1.48.

5   Ibbitson, "Older, longer."

6   Gordon Goldsborough. "Memorable Manitobans: Francis Alexander Lavens "Frank" Mathewson," accessed September 26, 2020, http://www.mhs.mb.ca/docs/people/mathewson_fal.shtml.

7   Robert B. Tate, T. Edward Cuddy, Francis A. L. Mathewson, "Cohort Profile: The Manitoba Follow-up Study (MFUS)," *International Journal of Epidemiology* 44, no. 5 (2015): 1528-1536, https://doi.org/10.1093/ije/dyu141.

8   Patrick Sullivan, "After 40 Years, RCAF Heart Study Still Flies as Participants Pay the Bills," *CMAJ* 141 (1989): 444-445, https://www.ncbi.nlm.nih.gov/pmc/articles/PMC1451397/pdf/cmaj00198-0086.pdf.

9   *The Manitoba Follow-up Study*, accessed September 27, 2020, http://mfus.ca/About.php.

10 Sullivan, "After 40 years," 444-445.

11 T. Edward Cuddy, Robert B. Tate, *The Manitoba Follow up Study – A Brief History* (Winnipeg: The Manitoba Follow-up Stud, 2000).

12 Sullivan, "After 40 years," 444-445; Cuddy and Tate, *The Manitoba Follow up Study*.

13 Tate, Cuddy, Mathewson, "Cohort Profile," 1528-1536.

14 Philip. D. St. John, Susan S. McClement, Audrey U. Swift, and Robert B. Tate, "Older Men's Definitions of Frailty – The Manitoba Follow-up Study," *Canadian Journal of Aging* 38, no. 1 (2019): 13-20, https://doi.org/10.1017/S0714980818000405.

15 Tate, Cuddy, and Mathewson, "Cohort Profile," 1528-1536; Francis Al Mathewson, Jure Manfreda, Robert B. Tate and T. Edward Cuddy, "The University of Manitoba Follow-up Study – An Investigation of Cardiovascular Disease with 35 Years of Follow-up," *Canadian Journal*

of *Cardiology* 3 (1987): 378-382; Robert. B. Tate, Jure Manfreda, Andrew Krahn, and T. Edward Cuddy, "Tracking of Blood Pressure Over a 40-Year Period in the University of Manitoba Follow-up Study, 1948–1988," *American Journal of Epidemiology*, 142, no. 9 (1995): 946–954, https://doi.org/10.1093/oxfordjournals.aje.a117742.

16   Robert B. Tate, Leedine Lah, and T. Edward Cuddy, "Definition of Successful Aging by Elderly Canadian Males: The Manitoba Follow-up Study," *Gerontologist* 43, no. 5 (2003): 735-744, https://doi.org/10.1093/geront/43.5.735; Robert. B. Tate, Brenda L. Loewen, Dennis J. Bayomi, and Barbara J. Payne, "The Consistency of Definitions of Successful Aging Provided by Older Men: The Manitoba Follow-up Study," *Canadian Journal of Aging*, 28, no. 4 (2009): 315-322, https://doi.org/10.1017/s0714980809990225; Robert B. Tate, Audrey U. Swift, and Dennis J. Bayomi, "Older Men's Lay Definitions of Successful Aging Over Time: The Manitoba Follow-up Study," *International Journal of Aging and Human Development*, 76, no. 4 (2013): 297-322, https://doi.org/10.2190/ag.76.4.b; Audrey U. Swift and Robert B. Tate, "Themes From Older Men's Lay Definitions of Successful Aging as Indicators of Primary and Secondary Control Beliefs Over Time: The Manitoba Follow-up Study," *Journal of Aging Studies*, 27 (2013): 410-418, https://doi.org/10.1016/j.jaging.2013.09.004.

17   St. John, McClement, Swift, and Tate, "Older Men's Definitions of Frailty," 13-20; Christian R. Hanson, Philip D. St. John, and Robert B. Tate, "Self-Rated Health Predicts Mortality in Very Old Men – the Manitoba Follow-up Study," *Canadian Geriatrics* Journal, 22, no. 4 (2019): 199-204, https://doi.org/10.5770/cgj.22.391; Christina O. Lengyel, D. Jiang, Robert B. Tate, "Trajectories of Nutritional Risk: The Manitoba Follow-up Study," *The Journal of Nutrition, Health & Aging*, 21 (2017): 604–609, https://doi.org/10.1007/s12603-016-0826-7.

18   Tate, Lah, and Cuddy, "Definition of Successful Aging by Elderly Canadian Males: The Manitoba Follow-up Study," 735-744.

19   Tate, Loewen, Bayomi, and Payne, "The Consistency of Definitions of Successful Aging Provided by Older Men: The Manitoba Follow-up Study," 315-322.

20   St. John, McClement, Swift and Tate, 13-20.

21   John W. Rowe and Robert L. Kahn, *Successful Aging* (New York: Pantheon, 1998).

22   Paul B. Baltes and Margaret M. Baltes "Psychological Perspectives on Successful Aging: The Model of Selective Optimization with Compensation," in P. B. Baltes and M. M. Baltes, editors, *Successful Aging: Perspectives from the Behavioral Sciences* (New York: Cambridge University Press: 1990), 1-34.

23   Sullivan, "After 40 Years," 444-445.

24 Andrew Bomback and Michelle Au, "Smartwatches Are Changing the Purpose of the EKG: Wearables Help Cast the Medical Test as a Talisman of Health-Care Competence. An Object Lesson," *The Atlantic,* February 17, 2019. Accessed September 27, 2020, https://www.theatlantic.com/technology/archive/2019/02/the-apple-watch-ekgs-hidden-purpose/573385/.

Acknowledgments

Thank you: Trevor Braem, Bob Petersen, Doug Curtis, Will Pratt, Clem Martini, Colleen Murphy, Anna Cummer, Kira Bradley, Chris Hunt, Kristen Padayas, Kathryn Kerbes, Sam MacDonald, Mark Bellamy, Michael Shamata, Karl Kjarsgaard, David Hogan, and Philip D. St. John.

Contributor Biographies

Photo Credit: Meg Braem

MEG BRAEM's plays have been nominated for a Governor General's Literary Award and won the Alberta Literary Award for Drama. She is a two-time winner of the Alberta Playwriting Competition. Meg's work has been presented at the Citadel Theatre, Theatre Calgary, The Belfry Theatre, Sage Theatre, Sparrow and Finch Theatre, Theatre Transit, Atomic Vaudeville, and Intrepid Theatre. She is a past playwright-in-residence at Workshop West Playwrights' Theatre and a member of the Citadel Playwrights Forum. Publications include *Blood: A Scientific Romance* (Playwrights Canada Press, 2013), *The Josephine Knot* (Playwrights Canada Press, 2018), and *Amplify: Graphic Narratives of Feminist Resistance*, co-authored with Norah Bowman and Dominique Hui (University of Toronto Press, 2019). Meg was the director of Alberta Theatre Projects' Playwrights Unit for two years and is a past Lee Playwright-in-Residence at the University of Alberta. She was the 2020/2021 Canadian Writer in Residence as part of the Calgary Distinguished Writer's Program at the University of Calgary. Most recently, Meg's play *The Resurrectionists* was produced by Larriken Entertainment and toured the Yukon.

DAVID B. HOGAN is a professor in the Division of Geriatric Medicine of the Cumming School of Medicine, University of Calgary.

PHILIP D. ST. JOHN is a professor of Geriatric Medicine at the University of Manitoba's Max Rady College of Medicine.

WILLIAM JOHN PRATT is an historian at Parks Canada.

SAMANTHA MACDONALD is a producer, director, and dramaturge who has been working in the theatre sector for over thirty years. She has had the good fortune to work for the National Arts Centre of Canada, Lunchbox Theatre, Inside Out Theatre, StoryBook Theatre, Theatre NorthWest, Project X Theatre Productions, and Western Canada Theatre to name a few. She was privileged to work with Meg Braem on the premiere production of *Flight Risk* as director and dramaturge.

BRAVE & BRILLIANT SERIES

SERIES EDITOR:
Aritha van Herk, Professor, English, University of Calgary
ISSN 2371-7238 (PRINT) ISSN 2371-7246 (ONLINE)

Brave & Brilliant encompasses fiction, poetry, and everything in between and beyond. Bold and lively, each with its own strong and unique voice, Brave & Brilliant books entertain and engage readers with fresh and energetic approaches to storytelling and verse.